The Re[...] Zachariah Kermit Higgins

A. S. Wood

To SHERLEY
HAVE A GREAT READ.
I HOPE YOU ENJOY THIS BOOK.

Wood
A. S.

Indigo Streams Publishing

Tulsa, Oklahoma

Explanatory

The spelling, grammatical, and punctuation errors observed and the abbreviations used in the Facebook messages are done to emulate the way kids communicate on Facebook.

Text copyright © 2017 by A. S. Wood.
Cover painted by © Mike Wimmer
Cover design by Jime Wimmer

Published by Indigo Streams Publishing
Indigostreamspublishing@gmail.com

Library of Congress Control Number: 2016920324
CreateSpace Independent Publishing Platform, North Charleston, SC

Author welcomes all input
Mail to: Indigostreamspublishing@gmail.com

Summary:
Seventh grader girls, Billie and Gem, fall for the guys of their dreams, Chad and Samson, on Facebook. As it turns out, these guys are none other than scrawny Zachariah, the classmate they have been bullying at school for months. Zach's quest for revenge by creating the online deception becomes a big confused knot that isn't working out like he planned, leading to unexpected outcomes.

ISBN-13: 978-1540788900
ISBN-10: 1540788903

[1. Bullying—Fiction. 2. Mother and son relationship—Fiction. 3. Facebook—Fiction. 4. Middle school—Fiction, 5. Family life—Fiction.]

Manufactured in the United States of America

CHAPTER 1

Monday, April 11

Looking like a large-footed stick figure in his white gym uniform, Zachariah Kermit Higgins lumbered to the gymnasium down the long hallway amidst a bunch of necks and shoulders. Although short, he wasn't the shortest kid in seventh grade, but he was the skinniest and the clumsiest.

As the thirteen-year-old got closer to the gym, his steps slowed down. He was in no hurry to get to P.E. class. When he shuffled his large feet into the gym, Mr. Doodash was taking roll.

"Jacob Williams."

"Present."

Zach slipped to the back row, his heart pounding.

"Yolanda Young."

"Present."

"Zach Higgins."

"Present," whispered Zach in a timid voice.

"Tardy," replied Mr. Doodash with a sigh. A wave of heat rushed from Zach's belly to the tip of his ears as his teacher added, "You need to move faster, buddy."

Immediately, Zach overheard a giggling Billie whisper, "His legs are too short." The kids within earshot emitted muffled laughs. Zach clenched his fists, wishing he could seal her lips with superglue. She always made everything worse.

Mr. Doodash blew his whistle, silencing the laughter.

The kids followed their teacher through the back door of the gym to the playground.

"Seems a good day for soccer," said Mr. Doodash. "Today, it's the girls' turn to be team captains."

He scanned the raised arms, choosing Yolanda and Billie.

Despite the balmy day and warm sun, Zach shivered. He had been hit with a double whammy, a team sport and Billie. Yolanda got the first pick. Of course, she chose Jack, the only boy in middle school who could wrestle high schoolers. Billie pouted and kicked the dirt with her foot but said nothing. She chose Antonio, one of the top players in their class.

The choosing continued.

"Byron."

"Summer."

"Kyle."

"Will."

The names rolled. Kids moved left and right to join their teams, leaving Zach behind until he stood alone. He wasn't surprised, but it still hurt. His hatred for gym class flared. It was humiliation hour for him and comedy hour for his classmates.

Billie's team still needed one more player. Zach was her only choice.

"Not fair," Billie screamed. She stomped her foot, her face beet-red. "Yolanda gets Jack, and I'm stuck with Zach Higgins."

Between Billie's outburst and the other students' muffled snickers and barely concealed smirks, Zach felt as unwanted as a chewed up and spat out bite of food. He fought hard to keep the accumulating tears from streaming down his cheeks.

"Each team has kids with different levels of abilities," said Mr. Doodash.

"Then Yolanda can take Higgins and give me one of her players."

Color drained out of Yolanda's face as she looked expectantly at Mr. Doodash.

"Enough. We're wasting precious time," said Mr. Doodash, throwing up his arms in exasperation. "This is gym class soccer, not the World Cup."

The game started. The kids chased the ball, each player trying to move it closer to his opponent's net. Everything seemed to move too fast and happen all at once. As usual, Zach felt lost and overwhelmed. One instant he'd see the ball in front of him, almost touching his foot. Every time he tried to kick it, his foot hit air while someone else's foot nailed it, moving it away from him.

At one point, the ball hit his foot. He kicked it and, for once, it rolled in front of him. *Yes,* he thought, *my foot made contact with the ball.* He ran after it. Competing with another foot, he kicked it again, more forcefully, in the direction of the net. Goal. As he basked in his triumph, his team jeered while the other team cheered. Nothing made any sense.

"You idiot!" Billie screamed at the top of her lungs. "You kicked the ball into our goal!"

Stunned, Zach stood immobile, drenched in the sweat of shame, wishing the earth would swallow him, or even better, he'd drop dead.

***

By lunchtime, the incident was all over the school. Kids laughed in his face and behind his back. In the cafeteria, Billie huddled with her friends. They talked, looking at him from time to time, making nasty faces when the teacher on lunch duty was at the other end of the room. Billie's mean actions were nothing new. For almost two years, Zach had suffered from her viciousness. She had repeatedly made cruel remarks about all kinds of things, especially his size, calling him names like "shorty," "midget," "klutzy," "wimpy," "stunted," and "dummy."

On his way to the fifth period, his foot caught on a shoe, and he stumbled. He swayed, extending his arms forward in an attempt to regain his balance. His teetering gradually slowed down until he steadied himself. Billie leaned against the wall, a smug smile on her face. Her canary yellow ballerina flats were unmistakably the shoes he tripped over.

When they went outside to catch their buses or rides, Billie was waiting for him by the front door.

"Hey, klutz," she yelled, "What moron kicks the ball into his own team's goal?"

He glanced quickly in her direction. Her disgusted face and angry eyes sent shudders down his spine. Agitated and aggravated, Zach walked into a crowd of students, hoping to lose her. For a moment, he thought he had gotten rid of her, but it took her no time to materialize next to him.

"You have no brain. Nothing. Nada," she shouted, the crowd's noise failing to drown her voice.

Zach felt himself shrinking and shrinking until he was the size of a bug. The sight of his bus parked at the end of the lot gave him some relief. He sped up. She followed, chanting, "Scrawny, stupid, spastic Zach doesn't know his front from back."

He ran as quickly as he could, but she chased him with her ditty for some distance, accompanied by the giggles, chuckles, and laughs of bystanders. Zach felt a mixture of shame and anger: shame for shooting the ball into the wrong net and anger for being tormented over it. After all, it was only gym class.

***

For the rest of the week, Zach tried to avoid Billie and her relentless insults but seemed to be running into her more than usual. Wherever he went, she turned up. He strongly suspected she was stalking him. Whenever there were no teachers, and they were within earshot, she chanted her nasty ditty, "Scrawny, stupid, spastic Zach doesn't know his front from back." Her song never lost its comical appeal to the other kids.

As the days passed, Zach's shame diminished while his rage flared until it reached the boiling point. Her latest actions had pushed him over the edge. He desperately wanted to avenge himself.

I'm going to teach Billie a lesson she'll never forget, he promised himself.

CHAPTER 2

Thursday, April 21

Here comes the Nag-a-Lot, thought Zach as his mother walked into the living room.

"Zachariah, are you done with your homework? Zachariah, I didn't hear you practice your fiddle. Zachariah, don't forget to practice your handwriting."

He wanted to tell his mother for the millionth time his name was *Zach*, but he knew she wouldn't budge. After all, his parents had named him after his mother's great-great-great grandfather who fought and died in the Civil War. Admittedly, that was cool, but not to the extent of being stuck with a name you'd see in a museum.

Zach also wanted for the millionth time to explain to his mother that the squeaky, screechy thing wasn't called a fiddle. It was called a violin when it was used to play the funeral music called "classical." And *nobody cares* about handwriting. His might be hard to read, but in five years, handwriting would be extinct. Practicing was a waste of time.

He nodded to his mom and half-smiled as if he were listening. Meanwhile, he calculated how quickly he could get to his room and get online. Tonight, he would finally launch his master plan against Billie, the Bully.

***

That evening, in the privacy of his room, Zach was about to launch a plot he was certain would teach Billie the lesson she'd never forget after two years of cruelty.

Zach had started to work on his plan last Sunday when he had Googled pictures of good-looking guys. A page full of photos had shown up. He had clicked on the first one. The guy had seemed promising but had been a bit too old. He had clicked on the second one, but Zach thought he was not the type Billie would fall for—not good-looking enough. The third kid was perfect. He had been the right age and had the looks Billie loved: sun-bleached blond hair, blue eyes, and a super body—the boy of choice for the plot. Zach had called him Chad. He had set up a Facebook account as Chad. Chad was a very accomplished athlete. He was a runner, a swimmer, and a soccer player. Just like Billie, he was a fan of Lady Gaga and Michael Jackson.

To make the Facebook account seem more realistic, he had recruited Patrick, his neighbor and best friend, to help him by providing a list of potential Facebook friends. Patrick was the ideal helper because he could keep a secret, and he went to a private Catholic school. He and Billie did not know each other and moved in separate social circles, making it unlikely they would have shared friends. The list didn't include any of Patrick's local friends to ensure absolute safety and secrecy. Instead, it included friends from summer camp in Wisconsin and from Chicago, where he regularly visited his grandparents. Zach had chosen a few from each group and had sent them requests to be his Facebook friends. All of them had accepted his friendship requests, probably, after Patrick encouraged them to accept the friendship of a guy named Chad.

Chad's Facebook account looked perfect and ready for Billie to be invited to join.

"Hello, Chad," Zach whispered to himself. "Goodbye, Zachariah."

He had a good feeling that she would accept Chad's friend request because he was good-looking and worth adding to her list of friends. The more popular Billie was, the happier she became. She was a sucker for these things, and Chad was going to be irresistible. Throughout the evening, Zach checked Chad's newsfeed regularly while he worked on his homework. Aside from a message from one of Patrick's Chicago friends about an old, rust-bucket jalopy he had seen in the parking lot of the mall, the site was inactive. No response from Billie.

***

"Zachariah!" yelled his mom from her room across the hall. "It's way past your bedtime."

With Billie always glued to her phone, there was a good chance she would still get his request on the same night. Zach set his alarm for 5:10 a.m. This would give him enough time to check for Billie's reply and hopefully, send her a message before getting ready for school.

"I still see lights," yelled his mother again.

Immediately, Zach turned off his lights and jumped into bed. He didn't want to provoke the suspicions of the Nag-a-Lot or her agent, his father. At that moment, how he wished he had brothers and sisters, preferably very young ones, to keep his parents too busy and off his back.

Zach tossed and turned in his bed, unable to fall asleep. Curiosity to find out Billie's response gnawed at him. With time, dread crept into his heart. He feared Billie would reject Chad's friend request, and his whole plan would fall apart. By midnight, he could not resist any longer. Quietly, he grabbed the flashlight from the drawer of his nightstand, walked to his desk, and checked Chad's Facebook. There was still no response from Billie.

Tired and disappointed, he returned to his bed and pulled his blankets over his head as if to hide from the whole world. This time, it did not take him long to fall into a very deep sleep. When his alarm rang, he turned it off and went back to sleep, his plan entirely forgotten.

Friday, April 22

A bright ray of sunshine assaulted his face as his mother's voice pierced his ears.

"Wake up! Wake up! It's almost 6:15."

He jumped out of bed and rushed through his morning routine when he suddenly remembered he needed to check his Facebook page, but it was too late. His simple flip phone was not connected to the Internet so he couldn't check on the bus.

CHAPTER 3

Friday, April 22, Continued

During the fifteen-minute ride to school, Zach thought of Billie and how in elementary school she shredded kids into pieces with her tongue and excluded them unless they showered her with praise or, for those who lacked the verbal talent, bribed her with services and gifts. He always pacified her with his homemade banana muffins. Nobody wanted Billie to unleash her tongue on them or exclude them, especially not from her two yearly super-awesome birthday parties when her divorced parents tried to outdo each other. In third grade, her dad and grandmother rented out Water Land Park and bussed the lucky invited kids, including him, for almost three hours to the park. After having the coolest water park all to themselves for three whole hours, they went to her grandmother's nearby house where they stuffed their faces with the tastiest snacks, cake, and ice cream. The following Saturday, her mom, in response to Billie's dad's treat, took the same group of lucky kids to a Harlem Globetrotters game, then to "Bounce-Bounce," where they jumped and bounced on gigantic inflatable bouncy castles for a whole hour before gorging on the best pudgy, fudgy cupcakes.

The bus pulled into its designated spot. Billie and her bratty cheerleaders were hanging out one or two yards away from the bus's door. Zach's heart sank. The kids rushed out. Zach remained seated, hoping the outpouring of students would dislodge Billie and her friends before he had to leave the bus. Unfortunately, they didn't move. He had no way out of greeting them; they were there right in his face. They totally ignored his greeting. He sighed and walked towards the school.

"Hey, scrawny monkey," yelled Billie at the top of her lungs as heads turned to see what the yelling was all about, "you look half your usual size. Did your mom shrink you in the dryer?"

The sound of laughter filled Zach's ears. His face felt hot. He wanted to say, "Hey, Billie, remember when you were fat and sat on Wal-Mart how all the prices went down?"

Instead, he said nothing, pretending not to hear and continued to walk towards the school. He wished the banana muffin still worked its magic. However, since the beginning of sixth grade when Billie returned from weight loss camp slim and fit, she lost interest in sweet offerings. Instead, she joined the school's dance club and started to hang out exclusively with the "cool kids." She not only excluded Zach but also launched a campaign of insults against him, becoming unbearable.

The thought of her impending punishment calmed him down. He hoped his plan would work. He wanted her to feel the same anguish that he was feeling between his ribs after two years of public ridicule.

He scurried down the hall in the direction of his locker to put his backpack away, grab a book, go to class, and bury his head in it, pretending to be reading.

Uh oh, he thought, stopping in his tracks. *What is the trio-of-terror doing so close to my locker?*

The "trio-of-terror," as Zach had nicknamed them, were Gem, their leader, Amanda, and Keisha. He had been avoiding this bunch since that Friday about a month ago when he had brought a ball to school to shoot hoops with his friends. When Gem had ordered him to give her the ball, he had refused. Gem had wrapped her arms around him from behind and had squeezed, forcing him to let go of the ball. He never saw that ball again. Zach thought of Gem as a real gangster, with her trademark faded black leather vest. She was tall, big-boned, and muscular, looking like an upright whale with long black, blond, and purple hair.

He thought perhaps if he tiptoed very quietly to his locker, they wouldn't pay attention to him. Wrong assumption! Zach felt choked as somebody grabbed the back of his collar.

"What are you doing in the hallway so early?" asked Gem.

"Just putting my backpack in my locker," mumbled Zach.

"I bet he's spying for Victoria and her gang," said Amanda.

"Why would I be spying for anybody?" he asked.

"Because you're scum," replied Keisha.

13

"Honestly, I'm putting away my backpack and grabbing a book. I have overdue homework I need to do."

"Liar," said Gem through clenched teeth as she impatiently pushed back the thick strand of blond hair hanging down the side of her face.

Gem slammed him against the lockers. Bang! Bang! Bang!

Zach saw Mrs. Jenson. He hoped she'd spot them and save him. Unfortunately, Gem saw Mrs. Jenson, too. She immediately stopped her assault and leaned against the locker while still maintaining a tight grip on his collar with the hand closest to the locker. She covered his mouth with her other hand as Keisha and Amanda quickly assembled next to her, forming a quarter-circle that concealed Zach. Totally oblivious to the incident, Mrs. Jenson walked happily into her classroom.

Gem slammed Zach against the lockers one more time.

"This is a warning," she said. "Never interrupt our meetings. Understand?"

"Yes, yes," he said in a shaky voice. "Just let me put my stuff away, and I'll never bother you again."

"Hurry up!"

He quickly placed his backpack in the locker and grabbed a couple of books.

"I'm done," he said. "As fast as lightning."

"Go to class, dummy," she said, shoving him away harshly. "This will get you to class even faster than lightning."

Zach tumbled onto the floor, palms first. He picked himself up to the tune of the gang's laughter. His scraped hands burned as if on fire.

As he walked to class, he wondered what her parents were thinking when they named her Gem. "Giantess," "Hulketta," "Monsteretta," "Elephante," or something like that would have been more appropriate. He felt sure her parents worked three jobs to keep her fed.

It was too bad that Mrs. Jenson did not catch Gem in action. At least, she would have spared him a slam and a shove. Complaining after the fact was pointless because nothing useful would come out of it. In sixth grade, he complained to the counselor when Nick, who thank goodness had moved to Alaska, beat him up and stomped on his lunchbox so hard that it broke. The counselor brought them to his office and gave them a lecture filled with nonsense talk about keeping their hands to themselves and off each other's things. Yeah, right. As a response to the counselor's advice, Nick kicked him soon after they left the office. Later in the year, he twisted his arm several times and once threw his backpack in a puddle of muddy water. Zach told his mom the backpack accidentally fell in the puddle so she wouldn't complain to the counselor, further complicating matters.

Between the pain of his scraped hands and his humiliated ego, Zach could not pay attention to anything all day.

***

Alone in his room after school, Zach collapsed on the bed and gazed at the ceiling for a long time. After what felt like a thousand years, he dragged himself to the computer and checked Chad's Facebook page. He almost jumped out of his seat. Hurray! Billie had accepted Chad's friend request. He immediately posted to her wall.

Chad
Thanx. Looked at all ur links. Awesome singer & dancer. Outfits soooo cool. Soooo impressed.

Just now

Everything Zach wrote in Chad's message was a bunch of lies. When Billie sang, she sounded like a choked-up crow. When she danced, she was kind of okay when the moves were simple, but she was clumsy when they got complicated. Her outfits were a cross between Dora the Explorer, a rock star, and Lil Wayne gone crazy. His goal was to make her feel good about herself, so she would fall deeper into the trap. Zach could not wait for her reply.

Emboldened by his success with Billie, he decided it was time for Gem to learn a lesson too. He wasn't sure how to approach her, but he figured since she was a girl, she'd like some boy attention. The trick was finding the right type of boy for her. Gem needed a tough boy. From school gossip, he knew she was on Facebook, but unlike Billie, whose Facebook account was public, Gem's was restricted only to her friends, leading many kids to spin rumors about her mysterious and possibly shady life outside of school.

Zach Googled the image of a tough guy. A photo of a boy

about fifteen or sixteen who was so muscular he didn't have a neck impressed him a lot. Zach felt he was the perfect type for Gem.

He didn't know what to call him. "Cliff," "Tough," "Rough," or what? Something was missing in all these names. They were too blunt. His name needed to reflect toughness because Gem was tough, but at the same time, it should be romantic in a way appealing to a girl like Gem.

At a loss, he sat frozen. Suddenly, the name "Samson" flashed inside his head. Yes, that fit the requirements exactly. Zach had just heard the story of Samson in church two Sundays ago. He was a super strong guy with long, curly hair who did not mind killing himself in the process of killing his enemies. Samson had a mind of his own just like Gem seemed to have. The kid in the photo had longish, curly hair, making the name Samson right for him.

Zach set up a Facebook account as Samson112. He had heard through the friend of a friend that Gem liked wrestling. So, of course, Samson liked wrestling. To be on the safe side, Zach added boxing, martial arts, football, and ice hockey. He then asked Gem and seven of the people on Patrick's list who were not Chad's Facebook friends to be Samson's friends.

***

Later in the evening, Zach checked both of his new Facebook pages just before going to bed. To his great delight, Gem had accepted Samson's friendship. He went to her Facebook page to give it a closer look. He didn't find anything except links and discussions about wrestling. She did not put much about herself. Her picture seemed to be taken from a distance and looked fuzzy. The only people who went to her Facebook page were her friends, Amanda and Keisha, providing wrestling links and contributing to the discussions.

Zach didn't know much about wrestling. He needed to educate himself. He decided YouTube was the best way to get a good and quick education. For a while, he surfed YouTube, looking for wrestling matches. In the first video, two wrestlers circled each other. The one in a red body suit and a red half-mask said, "You have no idea what El Diablo Rojo is gonna do."

"Beg to leave the ring in one piece?" replied the other

wrestler with a laugh as he ran his fingers through his shaggy blond hair.

El Diablo chuckled and said, "Gold, amigo, you're so wrong. I'm gonna rearrange your face. I'm gonna move your nose next to your ear. Then I'm gonna pull your bushy hair out by the roots and stuff it in your stinky mouth."

"Oh, really?" said Gold. "Well, I'm gonna throw you straight into the trashcan after I finish mopping the floor with you."

Suddenly, Gold grabbed El Diablo by the front of his bodysuit and pushed him into the ropes. He then swung his fist, targeting El Diablo's face. El Diablo moved to the side causing the blond wrestler to lose his balance. Before Gold managed to steady himself, El Diablo dealt him several punches to the stomach in quick succession, causing him to double over. As the beaten up wrestler staggered, El Diablo pushed him. Gold fell face down to the ground. Immediately, El Diablo threw himself over Gold and pulled his hair with one hand and used the weight of his body and the other hand to pin him in place. The referee started to count, "One, two, three…" By the count of four, Gold kicked the floor forcefully, releasing himself from El Diablo's grip.

Zach clicked on another link. He saw a wrestler with long, black, oily hair shoving another wrestler into the ropes. He then ran at him and kneed him as a deep voice announced, "Smith delivers his famous knee kick."

"I know it's Friday," yelled his mom from her room, interrupting his attempt to continue his wrestling education. "Still, you need to go to bed at a decent time."

"We don't want our sleep to get shifted over the weekend," added his dad.

Ordinarily, Zach would have argued and tried to squeeze out another hour, but for the sake of the plan, he decided to play obedient.

"I guess you're right," he whined, trying not to arouse her suspicion by being too obedient.

"Not," he hissed angrily to himself as he caught a glimpse of the two wrestlers engaged in a punching match.

"Oh, I'm so glad and proud you finally came to your senses," his mother said.

Hearing the thump of her feet, he barely managed to log out

of YouTube before she stormed into his room and wrapped her arms around him.

"Couldn't you at least knock before rushing in?" he retorted, without returning her hug.

"I got too excited. I forgot," she said, moving her arms away. "I'll try to remember to knock next time. I promise."

He quietly nodded his head. Trying to remember was the most she could promise. Deep down, Zach was sure his mom's idea of privacy was fuzzy at best. He must be alert at all times because she could never be trusted to knock on the door. No matter how many times she promised and how good her intentions were, she'd likely slip and forget.

"Goodnight, sweetie. Can I have a real hug now?"

"Goodnight," he said, gently hugging her, hoping the hug would put an end to her unwanted visit.

CHAPTER 4

Saturday, April 23

The Nag-a-Lot always ruins everything, thought Zach throughout the morning as his mother dragged him from one store to another. She was looking for the best deal on a new pair of shoes for him—not that he urgently needed new shoes, but just because it was the weekend of bargains at the mall. Again, he wished he had, like normal kids, a smartphone. Then, at least, he could have checked the Facebook walls of all of his selves during the half-hour drive. His mother did not think a thirteen-year-old needed such a phone. A simple phone for emergencies was good enough.

When they finally arrived home with the best bargain his mother could find, Zach rushed to his room.

"Have some lunch," his mom boomed as soon as his hand touched the doorknob. "Zachariah, you must be hungry and dehydrated just like me."

"Later, Mom."

"There's no such thing as later. You only had a small breakfast."

Zach figured obedience was the shortest way to a peaceful afternoon. He wore the new shoes, smiled, and washed down his dry turkey sandwich with large amounts of lemonade.

Finally, when he was in his room, he immediately went to Chad's Facebook page and followed the link to Billie's wall.

Billie P.
check out my performance of thriller

                                                                    4 hours ago

Boy, he could have seen that message hours ago had it not

been for his mother.

He clicked on Billie's video.

Dang. What a way to butcher Thriller, he thought. He had to admit that with her sleepy face and messy hair, she looked like she just got out of the grave.

She got a small part of the song right. The rest was a disaster.

He browsed through the comments.

Liz, Billie's sort of best friend, commented,

Liz Cooper
So-so. Michael Jackson's version my fav

2 hours ago

Steve, Billie's boyfriend, a football player from the most expensive private school in town, as usual, thought whatever she did was wonderful.

Wow, thought Zach. *He's either blind or a big liar.*

Now it was time for Chad to formulate the biggest lie of them all. Before he typed his comment, Billie replied to Liz's comment.

Billie P.
OMG his performance is like sooo yesterday while mine is totally 21st century ur taste stink

2 seconds ago

That's Billie, Zach thought. *As cocky as can be.*

Zach typed Chad's reply.

Chad
Awesome video. loved it sooooooooo much. Ur version is the bomb.

Just now

He pressed the send button, then went to YouTube, where he spent the rest of the afternoon watching wrestling videos. A few of the clips he found seemed interesting, and he sent Gem one of them. In that clip, a massive muscular man with a shaved head and white-streaked red beard stood inside the ring, sneering and flexing his muscles. Two men climbed into the ring. One was wearing black tights and a black mask. The other was dressed in a shirtless formal suit.

"Grandpa, the party is over," said the man in the suit. "Go home to your plastic girlfriend."

Viewers in the arena, holding signs with "Celtic Shawn" printed on them in large letters, booed.

The masked man pointed at the audience and yelled, "You're just like him—losers."

"I'm getting mad," roared Celtic Shawn, his voice rough. "Madder than I've ever been."

"Mad, shmad," said the man in the suit with a laugh. "Run before Big Hulk crushes your bones."

"Ouch, I'm so scared," said Celtic Shawn with a laugh, ", you're just a piece of rotten garbage."

The audience waved their signs and chanted, "Celtic Shawn, Celtic Shawn, Celtic Shawn…"

Big Hulk took off his mask while his companion removed his jacket, revealing a muscular upper body. A third muscular man slipped under the ropes into the ring. Big Hulk wrapped his massive, muscular arms around Celtic Shawn's chest as each of the other two men grabbed a leg. Celtic Shawn thrashed around, attempting to free himself, but he was overpowered by the three men who lifted him and threw him into the arena as Big Hulk screamed, "You want him. Grab him." Celtic Shawn landed on a group of spectators. As he gathered himself and stood up, he farted. Within a few seconds, the disgusted nearby spectators ran off in different directions with their noses pinched. One man even puked in a nearby trashcan.

Sunday, April 24

Neither Chad nor Samson received any updates until the evening when Billie posted a message on her wall. Although so far she had not directly replied to any of his messages, at least she had accepted his friendship.

Billie P.
Lunch tacos at Fluffy's mmmmhhhhh ♡ tacos
18 minutes ago

Yuck. Zach couldn't stand Mexican food, but, of course, he could mold Chad on demand.

Chad
NO WAY! Will have TACOS 4 dinner 2. Already smacking my lips.

Just now

There was no post from Gem regarding his wrestling link, but Keisha and Amanda hated it. They thought it was mostly silly dissing and clowning and not much wrestling. Fearing Gem's reaction could be just as negative, his heart sank. She'd lose interest in him, and his plan would go down the toilet. Disappointed, he decided not to send the YouTube link he had planned on posting.

Monday, April 25

Zach arrived home late due to the combination of Robotics Club and a rush hour traffic jam on the highway. Eager to check his various Facebook accounts, he threw his backpack and lunchbox on the hallway floor and rushed to his room. Before he even touched the mouse, his mom knocked on the door.

"Dinner time," she shouted as if a street block separated them.

"In a minute."

"Fine."

He clicked on the mouse hurriedly and repeatedly, causing the computer to jam and slow down.

"Stupid computer!" he murmured.

On the screen, the lower part of the hourglass filled slowly.

"Hurry, hurry!" he hissed, cheering it on.

Finally, the Google page appeared on the screen, and the computer was normal again.

No updates for Chad.

"Your minute is over," yelled his mother from behind the closed door.

Fumbling to go to Samson's page, he didn't reply.

"It's that darn computer," she said with impatient anger.

"Zachariah Kermit Higgins, if you don't get out of your room this instant, you are going to lose access to it for a very long time."

Zach jumped out of his seat in response to the threat and followed his mother to the kitchen.

"Why all this hurry?" he asked.

"I need to get dinner over with because I have to be at work early tomorrow. Dr. Jackson starts his surgeries at 6:30 sharp."

Zach sat glumly at the dinner table as his mother ladled chili onto their plates.

"I admire Dr. Jackson so much," she said. "On Saturday, he'll travel to Africa where he'll spend two weeks doing charity work, operating on people with badly damaged hands."

"He's a great man," said Zach's father. "It's a shame you won't be working with him when you move across the street to the heart hospital."

"I'll surely miss him," she said wistfully, shaking her head in agreement while buttering her roll. "What can I do? Couldn't turn down the offer."

"Anyway, the new hours will work better for our family," said his father, dowsing his wife's mild chili with hot sauce. "The pay raise won't hurt us either."

For a while, they ate silently.

"Put the iPod down," snapped Zach's mom. "How many times have I told you not to play with electronics while we're eating?"

"But I'm bored," protested Zach.

"Bored?" shouted his mother. "Nonsense. This is the time of day when we sit down as a family and have conversations. We are supposed to talk about our day and interesting things that happened to us."

"Nothing interesting happened to me," said Zach.

"Well, then me and your dad will talk about our days."

Here she goes again, thought Zach. He knew what she'd be gabbing about. She'd analyze every surgeon she works with—the same surgeons and the same analyses. His Dad would be talking about all of the long and boring accounting meetings he had to sit through. Since they were going to either be silent or talk about the same old stuff, Zach didn't understand why he couldn't play with his iPod. His mom doesn't get anything.

"Zachariah, why didn't you eat the artichoke and beet salad

today? It returned in your lunchbox untouched."

"Not very hungry."

"Well, it's because you start with the dessert. Next time, make sure you start with your salad. If you get too full, then you'll bring back the dessert."

"I'll try."

"You'd better try for real. Otherwise, no desserts in your lunchbox."

Zach thought his mom didn't understand how embarrassing it was for him to pull out the transparent container from his lunchbox and then pick those strange looking things and eat them in front of everybody. He wondered why she couldn't hide them inside fries or nuggets so nobody could see them.

"Zachariah, why are you scattering your super fruits all over the plate?" asked his mother.

"I don't like them. They're squishy."

"They're a bit overripe. Blueberries are expensive. I was very lucky to find them on sale. Take advantage of this bargain."

Zach grunted in protest.

"Don't be so picky. Children in Africa are dying from starvation," added his father.

That's what I have to live with every day of my life, thought Zach.

***

When he finally was back in his room, to his delight, Gem had sent Samson a private message.

Gem Bardel

Loved your YouTube video. I like your sense of humor. Send me more videos.

Don't pay any attention 2 my friends. I will agree with them. I don't want 2 hurt their feelings.

43 minutes ago

Immediately, he replied.

Samson 112
Happy u loved my video. Will send u 1 every day. I
promise.

Just now

CHAPTER 5

Tuesday, April 26

The school's baseball team was having its annual ice cream fundraiser. Zach, the chocolate monster, bought a chocolate ice cream bar dipped in a thick dark chocolate coating. He unwrapped it carefully, his saliva flowing with every crinkle of the wrapper. Too absorbed in his task, he did not notice Gem moving in his direction until she loomed over him.

"Ooh, what yummy flavor did you get?" she said, pointing to the ice cream bar.

Cold sweat ran down his back.

"Double chocolate," he said, his voice slightly shaky.

"My favorite!" she said with gusto as she extended her arm. "I want it."

"Go get your own. They're selling them for $3.00."

"I forgot my money at home."

"Not my problem," he said, trying hard to keep his voice steady in an attempt to cover up his fear.

"Give it nicely," she hissed through clenched teeth, "or you're going to pay when no teachers are looking."

Reluctantly, he gave her the ice cream bar and walked away quickly, his heart heavy with disappointment for losing his bar and anger for failing to stand up to her.

Wednesday, April 27

School was out for teachers' professional training day. When Zach checked Chad's Facebook in the evening, he found a post from Billie.

Billie P.
OMG golden paradise bestest movie ever
girl star just like me.beautiful smart sensitive ☺

4 hours ago

"Yeah, right," whispered Zach, rolling his eyes. He then started to look at the responses. One response caught his eye.

Jana DeFelice
Excuse me. U sensitive, NO WAY. Movie stinks.

3 hours ago

Jana and Billie were an odd pair. They were on/off friends because they got on each other's nerves.

Billie P.
jana u know 0 about sensitivity

3 hours ago

Steve Barber
Jana don't be mean. Billie IS VERY sensitive.

3 hours ago

Jana DeFelice
I know a lot about sensitivity and honesty too.

2 hours ago

Wow, thought Zach. *Things are heating up.*

Billie P.
STOP hating on me

2 hours ago

Jana DeFelice
Not hating on u. u want way too much. Can't say wow to everything u say or do. I'm unfriending u!

About 1 hour ago

Billie P.
cool don't need ur negativity.

40 minutes ago

The other comments came from Billie's close friends. Of course, they praised both her and the movie and condemned what they called Jana's "negativity." Although Zach agreed wholeheartedly with Jana, Chad needed to outdo all of Billie's friends, especially Steve.

Chad
Golden Paradise **is awesome. Don't personally know u, but from ur messages and links, I know u r beautiful smart sensitive Talented. Jana has an attitude problem.**
Glad she left.

Just now

Friday, April 29

Billie posted a link to another performance on her wall. Again, Chad praised it. Aside from her horrible voice, her dancing was all right. At least, this time, his lie was a bit smaller.

Saturday, April 30

Zach's mom was working in the hospital, and his father was watching golf on TV, giving Zach plenty of time to think. He decided Chad had flattered Billie enough without even getting a direct response to any of his posts. It seemed things were going nowhere with her. Chad was just one of her gazillion Facebook friends, and he needed to distinguish himself from the rest. It was time for a bolder approach. It was riskier but unavoidable if he was to get anywhere with Billie.

CHAPTER 6

Saturday, April 30, continued

Chad
U r hot smart and talented. Always thinking about u. Want 2 b ur boyfriend.

Just now

Zach sent it as a private message and then sat gazing at the screen, waiting for a response. Within a few minutes, Billie replied with another private message.

Billie P.
WOW OMG I already have a boyfriend silly

38 seconds ago

Oops, he thought. *I must have moved too fast. I should apologize and then move a little slower.*

However, keeping the whole thing private was a promising sign. Zach knew Billie well enough to be sure she could have easily rejected Chad publicly to brag about her desirability, totally ruining the plot in the process.

He sent her another private message.

Chad
Sorry, my bad. U r soooo irresistible. I like wasn't thinking straight.

Just now

As soon as he sent the message, he logged off. During the

afternoon, he helped his father change the office's doorknob then played video games with Patrick.

Sunday, May 1

Zach checked Chad's Facebook as soon as he woke up from a restless sleep. He found a private message from Billie, where she had accepted his apology. Under the message was a big yellow smiley face.

***

As promised, Zach had every day been posting a link to a wrestling video he deemed funny onto Gem's Facebook. Keisha, Amanda, and Gem made fun of his videos and his sense of humor. Again, they thought his choices were full of dissing, monkeying around and gymnastics with little wrestling. Gem, however, continued to send private messages, praising his choices and asking for more. He was happy. He had been able to keep her interest going. At the same time, he was confused about her. He felt she was contradictory. On her public Facebook wall, she said one thing, and in her private messages, she said the exact opposite. It seemed she was kind of like him—trying to be two people at the same time. The only difference between them was that he did not think she had a plan in mind. She was simply thinking naturally with no hidden intentions other than, maybe, pleasing everybody.

Zach needed to find new videos, but as soon as he started looking on YouTube, his mother yelled from behind his door.

"Breakfast is ready. Church in forty minutes. You need to be in the kitchen in no more than ten minutes."

"I'm tired. Can I take a break from church?"

"No."

"Please. I'm really very tired."

"I never liked having that computer in your room. Maybe we should move it to the living room, so it won't be a constant temptation, depriving you of sleep and keeping you tired."

"Okay," he said, dissatisfaction apparent in his voice.

***

After lunch, he ran straight to his room and logged onto Samson's Facebook where he found a private message from Gem that had nothing to do with wrestling.

Gem Bardel
Love your taste and sense of humor when choosing your wrestling videos. I think I like U. U must not be from stupid Pine City. I hate Pine City. We never had a good day since we moved here. This freaking city is all bad luck.

32 minutes ago

Immediately, he replied that he was from New York City. His mother grew up only a few hours outside the city, and every two years, they go back for a family reunion at the farm where her parents still live. Sometimes, they spend a couple of days in the city when the reunion is over. So, he was kind of from there. Her reply was prompt as if she had expected a quick response and was waiting to have a conversation.

Gem Bardel
Thought so. NYC is a cool place. I've never been there and I don't think I'll ever go there. It's expensive and we're 2 poor.

13 seconds ago

Aha, Zach thought. *Gem is a poor girl.* He should already have figured that out. Bus 318 went to the dumpy part of town. He was probably the last one in school to figure that out. What a doofus!

He sent her another message.

Samson112
Want 2 tell me about ur bad luck?

Just now

Gem Bardel
I feel more comfortable sharing with U than anybody else cuz you live far away. My story won't be all over school.

Maybe I'll tell U some other time. Don't get me wrong. I'm not ready yet.

16 seconds ago

Zach felt triumphant as Gem opened up, even partially. Soon he might learn something about her that would help him with his revenge. However, he also felt sad and sorry for Gem, something he had never felt for Billie even though he had known her since kindergarten. Billie was always interested only in herself and always wanted something from others, but Gem seemed like a very sad girl. In her private messages, she didn't seem tough or mean at all, but quite nice and gentle as if the toughness he saw in school was a shell to ward off more bad luck.

Monday, May 2

Throughout the week, every day, Billie sent Chad a private message, consisting of a big yellow smiley face without any words. On her wall, she was unusually inactive. Samson continued sending Gem a link to a funny wrestling clip every day and receiving the same kind of responses, negative in public and positive in private.

Friday, May 6

Gem's private message was purely personal.

CHAPTER 7

Friday, May 6, Continued

Gem Bardel

I'm the oldest of 4, George, 11, Jim, 10, and Gina, 7. I'll turn 14 in July. Before we came 2 Pine City, we lived in a small town in Minnesota. We had a big house, a big yard, and a big dog called Ginger. My dad owned a mechanic shop and my mom was a supervisor in a cheese factory. We were happy.

When I was in grade 4, my parents started thinking about moving 2 Pine City. Dad wanted 2 be close 2 his old mother cuz he is her only child. He found a job in a car repair shop and we moved here in the middle of September. We enrolled in Adam's Elementary 2 weeks late. My mom started 2 look 4 a job. It took forever 2 get used 2 the hugeness of Pine City. I'm sure it is a speck compared 2 NYC.

The houses in Pine City were more expensive than in Minnesota, so we ended up buying a smaller house. It was still a nice house with a beautiful yard. Instead of having our own rooms, the boys shared a room and me and Gina shared another. The neighborhood park was close. We took Ginger there a lot and she was happy.

About 1 hour ago

There was nothing much in this message to help him with his revenge, but he figured the best thing to do was to make her comfortable so she'd continue to open up. One day, she would spill out some deep, dark secret, and he would get her.

Samson 112
That's hard. I'd be sad if my parents moved out of New

York. I think I'd die from sadness. u r brave.
 Yeah, New York is huge.

Just now

Saturday, May 7

Billie sent a link to YouTube where she showed off stuff she had bought during a shopping spree: a glittery, pink lip gloss and a pair of flip-flops with golden straps.
 Zach, as Chad, posted on her wall.

Chad
Lovely, sparkly things. Match ur personality.

Just now

Of course, she got lots of compliments from her friends. That was what friends were for according to Billie; to praise you whenever you did anything you thought was important enough to post on your Facebook page.

Monday, May 9

There were more daily private messages from Billie with big, yellow smiley faces. However, that week, they were winking ones. Zach could not figure out what all those winking and non-winking smiley faces were supposed to mean. Billie was starting to get on his nerves. Gem kept on ridiculing his wrestling videos in public without mentioning them in private.

Monday, May 9, Continued

Gem sent Samson a private message.

Gem Bardel
 Except 4 Grandma Cordelia, we didn't know anybody in this nasty city. People in this stinky city didn't seem 2 like outsiders. They waved at us from their driveways before going inside and locking their doors. Despite the nice weather, they never sat on their front porches. High wooden fences

surrounded their backyards. Whenever we'd run into them in the park playing with their dogs or children, they'd huddle together and stay away from us like we had cooties. We missed the people from our town. We missed the piles of snow. We missed making snow angels and building big snowmen with long orange noses and mismatched button eyes. We missed ice skating on frozen ponds. We missed ice fishing. The weather here is different. In Pine City, the little bit of snow we get melts in a day.

11 hours ago

"She misses big piles of snow," whispered Zach to himself. "What a weirdo!"

Of course, Samson was not allowed to think like Zach. Thank goodness, Billie and Gem were into different things. Otherwise, he wouldn't have been able to keep track of what Chad and Samson loved and hated, and what they were allowed to think and say. Despite that, he was starting to feel things getting jumbled inside his head.

Samson 112

Love snow soooo much and wish we got more of it in the city. Wish we spent the winter in upstate NY where they get tons of snow. It's a bummer u can't enjoy it anymore. On top of that, u have 2 deal with mean people.

Just now

Wednesday, May 11

Zach did not have a chance to log onto his computer until late in the evening. His great aunt Agnes dropped by to introduce her new husband, Rudolph. His mom insisted they stay for dinner. Of course, he had to be the perfect good boy and hang out with the eighty-something newlyweds.

"Oh, Zachariah, you have grown so much since I last saw you," was the first thing Aunt Agnes said as soon as she saw him, which was, of course, the first thing she always said whenever she saw him. This time, at least, she did not pinch his cheek, but she still gave him a partially melted fun-sized chocolate bar from her purse's snack compartment, where she kept a stash of chocolate and sweets in case she felt faint or light-headed which she felt quite often. No wonder she was the same size vertically and horizontally.

Thank goodness, Aunt Agnes had a strict bedtime of 8:30, so they didn't stay very long after dinner. Zach was able to go to his room as soon as he finished loading the dishwasher while his mother cleared the table.

***

He first checked Samson's Facebook page where he found a private message full of unexpected and shocking surprises.

CHAPTER 8

Gem Bardel

Freaking Adam's Elementary is the smallest school in Pine City. Has only 2 sections 4 each class. The kids have known each other since kindergarten.

During the first month of school, some nasty children threw trash in my locker several times, spilled nail polish all over my backpack, and spray-painted my legs through the lower part of the bathroom door when I was sitting on the toilet. I suspected some kids but could not prove anything.

During lunch, all my classmates made sure 2 leave 3 or 4 seats between me and them. I always ate lunch surrounded by empty seats. Freaking Adam's Elementary was like hell. On my way there every morning, I felt more and more nauseous the closer I got 2 it.

3 hours ago

He reread the message, his jaw dropping further with every sentence.

"Gem was bullied," he repeated to himself in disbelief.

He wondered how he should reply. He was not allowing Samson to be a victim of bullying. Samson would give her lots of sympathy, but that's as far as he'd allow him to go, no matter what. At least for once, Zach could be bullying-proof, even if it were only through Samson.

Samson 112

What a bunch of mean ugly jerks. Nobody ever bullied me, but my short and skinny friend is bullied a lot. When I'm around, they don't bully him cuz I always come 2 his rescue. They attack him when I'm not around. Feels 2 him school is like torture land. He keeps it all 2 himself. I think his mom suspects kids are making fun of his size. She tells him he's a late bloomer, just like his dad. One day, he'll start growing like a bean stalk. If he does some push-ups and sit-ups he'll develop muscles and won't look so skinny.

And suppose he stays short and scrawny. What's the big deal? People come in different shapes, sizes, colors, and with different features. All that shouldn't matter.

Just now

Zach sent the message, his ears burning and his whole body sweating, wishing Samson were a real person who always came to his rescue. Unfortunately, his friends were all outcasts, just like him.

Zach checked Chad's Facebook page. Billie's private message was still the silly winking smiley face. On her public Facebook page, she had a YouTube link where she showed off stuff she had bought on sale—a pair of boots and a pair of very short shorts. She disappeared behind a curtain. When she reappeared, she was wearing her shorts and boots. She threw her head up in the air and twirled around as she sang, "These boots are going to walk all over you."

Again he praised the outfits and the performance but thought, *What a bore!*

All of a sudden, he felt exhausted and very sleepy. The whole day felt muddled inside his head: eighty-four-year-olds eloping to Jamaica, a bullied bully, and a master plan leading nowhere except to the private world of smiley faces with different expressions and public silly self-centered links. A worn-out Zach barely managed to drag himself to bed without even taking off his clothes. Following that weird evening, he stopped logging onto the Internet.

Friday, May 13

The whole school was buzzing with Billie's previous night's Facebook wall post.

Oh, how stupid of me, thought Zach. *Why did I stop checking? I won't have access to Facebook until I go home.*

His friend, Logan, the gossip king, was nowhere to be found. When he bumped into his younger sister, she told him Logan had a stomach bug. What luck!

CHAPTER 9

Friday, May 13, Continued

Zach acted uninterested in all the frenzy but went around eavesdropping. Soon, he overheard two girls talking. Billie broke-up with Steve. She left him for Chad because he was cooler.

Bingo, he thought. *All the praise did something after all.* A surge of happiness bolted throughout his body like lightning and took him to another world, making him unaware of his surroundings.

"Get out of the way, you scrawny retard!" he heard Billie scream. "You're blocking the way. What's wrong with you?"

With a smile, he moved to the side, allowing her to pass.

***

As soon as Zach got home, he rushed to his bedroom and went straight to Billie's wall.

Billie P.

me & steve r no longer together he's immature & like doesn't appreciate me & is a jerk. I'm now in a new better relationship with chad he's mature always soooo supportive my big fan totally COOL chad is my soul mate XOXOXO ♡ ♡♡
☺☺☺☺☺☺☺

21 hours ago

Zach read Billie's post several times for the sheer enjoyment. His grin widened with every reread word until it turned into uncontrolled laughter, almost hysterical as he repeatedly slapped his thigh, his eyes glistening with tears.

There were lots of replies and comments about the breakup, but he did not care to read any of them. The sweet moment of revenge was getting closer. That was all he cared about.

He posted a reply on her wall.

Chad

Sooo happy we r now a couple. I always felt we were soul mates 2.

Just now

On Samson's Facebook page, he found a private message from Gem.

Gem Bardel

U have a good heart.

U know, your small friend reminded me of a boy I beat up at my school. Maybe I shouldn't have done that, but I'm sure he was spying 4 this girl, Victoria, my archenemy. My friend, Keisha, is with them in the same science class and saw them swapping notes.

Zach was furious.

He and Victoria swapping notes, he thought. *How crazy!* Didn't Keisha know that Victoria and Trish sat next to each other at the beginning of the year? Didn't Keisha know that two weeks later, Mr. Smith put Zach between them after he got fed up with their nonstop chatter? They had stopped talking but started passing notes through Zach. Who would dare say no to Victoria? She's ten times nastier than Gem.

After he had calmed down a little, he resumed reading Gem's message.

Let's forget about the boy and continue my story in stupid Pine City. I hope I'm not boring u with my story.

3 days before Christmas, my dad was driving home at night. 2 save time, he took a back road. The driver of a big truck ran a red light and crashed into my dad's car. The driver drove away and left my dad badly injured. The passengers of a passing car saw a wrecked car and found him. They called 911. My dad had 2 stay in the hospital for 6 days. Merry Christmas 2 us!

All his injuries healed except his right hand. What use is

a mechanic without 2 good hands? His only hope was an operation 2 fix his hand. He did not have health insurance & couldn't afford the surgery.

Dad was stuck at home with a bad hand, had no job, no health insurance, and no money, and a gazillion medical bills to pay. He became cranky and gloomy and spent most of his time in his room with the door locked. My mom got a job at Yummy Hamburgers but was making little money.

The whole atmosphere at home changed. My dad lived in his own world. My mom was exhausted and always fighting tears. The boys stopped paying attention at school and became loud and obnoxious at home. Gina became super quiet. We stopped doing things together as a family cuz we weren't really a family anymore with my dad locked in his room, my mom working strange hours, and my sister and brothers turning into weirdos. We also had no money 2 pay 4 all the fun activities we used 2 do like movies, bowling, and karate lessons. Sometimes, we were not even able 2 pay our bills. Our phone was disconnected once. Our power was almost disconnected, but my mom pawned her wedding ring 2 pay the bill.

19 hours ago

Zach was tangled with his creations, Chad and Samson, in what seemed like a big confused knot. Chad was happy as he was supposed to be. After all, he got his girl. Zach was happy because his plan against Billie was on track. It was only a matter of time before he delivered the final blow.

While the first part of Gem's message angered Zach, the remainder made him sad. It was normal to be angry when she falsely accused him of exchanging notes with Victoria and spying for her. Feeling sorry for Gem, however, didn't make sense. Not long ago, she forced his ball out of his hands, she banged him against the lockers and shoved him mercilessly, and she intimidated him into giving her his ice cream bar. He should be sad about his inability to find a way to get at her, not sad about her misfortunes. Of course, Samson was supposed to be heartbroken over her hardships. Samson also should not show much interest in a puny boy so far away in Pine City. Or should he? Maybe Samson could have a little difference in opinion with Gem about the puny kid without risking the disruption of his plan. He started to type.

Samson 112
Ur stories do not bore me at all. Want 2 know more. Pine City has been full of suffering 4 u and ur family. Ur story broke my heart. Hate Pine City without ever being there. Admire ur courage sooo much. Hang in there girl. Hope things will get better.

Still thinking about the boy. Maybe u were a bit 2 quick in judging him, and he didn't deserve 2 be beaten up.

Just now

***

When Zach checked Chad's Facebook page after dinner, he found a private message from Billie. She wanted to go out on a date to the movies or the bowling alley over the weekend.

His heart sank. Of course, Billie would want to meet up with her boyfriend, but he had not thought of that detail when he put his plan together. Where was he going to come up with the kid in the photograph and convince him to play the role of Chad? What was he going to do? A couple of weeks was all he needed before delivering the final blow.

As he sat frozen in front of the computer, trying to figure out how to evade a face-to-face meeting with Billie, he heard loud knocking on the front door and his mother's hurried footsteps down the hall. Some murmuring followed. Zach could not determine who his mother was talking to, or what was going on.

"Zachariah," his mom yelled. "Mrs. Marvin is hurt. I need to go check on her."

Zach continued to gaze stupidly at his screen, his heart racing, his palms sweating. A few moments later, he heard the siren of an ambulance. Something interesting must be happening at the Marvin's. Since he was still stuck in his mess, he decided to check out what was going on. He logged out and ran to the Marvin's house.

***

All the action was in the garage. Mrs. Marvin lay on the floor next to a toppled ladder, her gray hair disheveled, her wrinkled face strained with pain. She moaned softly as one paramedic examined her.

"She was standing on the ladder changing the light bulb," said Mr. Marvin. "I heard a loud thump and a scream. I ran here where I found her on the floor crying. A tough gal like her doesn't cry easily. She must have been in great pain."

"I think her arm is broken," said the paramedic after questioning Mrs. Marvin and examining her. "We need to take her to the hospital for some tests."

The two paramedics put her carefully on a stretcher and carried her to the back of the ambulance. Mr. Marvin climbed into the back of the ambulance with the help of Zach's mom.

"Call me when you know something, or you're ready to come home," Mrs. Higgins said. "I'll come pick you up."

A dazed Mr. Marvin quietly nodded his head.

The ambulance left the neighborhood slowly and noiselessly. Distraction over! Zach still had not figured out a way to delay a meeting between Chad and Billie for the next two weeks. His heart pounded violently.

***

Zach moved restlessly from room to room, trying to avoid his bedroom.

"Zachariah," his mother said, "it's past your bedtime."

"Please let me stay up a little longer."

"Poor baby. You must be worried about Mrs. Marvin."

"Yes, yes," he said absently.

"They are such wonderful neighbors. I'll make an exception tonight until we hear from them."

"Thank you," he said, feeling relieved.

He turned on the TV and pretended to watch some program about space. His mother sat next to him. Some time later, the phone rang. Zach gazed at the TV as his mother left the room to answer the phone.

"Yup, she broke her arm," she said when she returned to the living room. "It's all taken care of now. The poor lady won't be able to use her arm or drive for at least four weeks."

Bingo! A light bulb lit inside Zach's head.

"I'm going to bring them back home," added his mother, interrupting his train of thought. "Would you like to come?"

"I'm exhausted," said Zach, faking a long, noisy yawn. "I'd better go to sleep."

"Alright, I should be back shortly."

Zach shuffled to his room, pretending to be very sleepy. As soon as he was all by himself, he quickly logged onto Chad's Facebook and accepted to go to the movies with Billie on Sunday afternoon.

Everything is going to be all right, thought Zach as he drifted off to sleep.

CHAPTER 10

Saturday, May 14

Around noon, Zach wrote Billie a private message.

> **Chad**
> **OMG mom fell off the ladder, broke right arm. No driving 3–4 weeks. So upset. Have no ride 2 theater. Live out in the country, 30 miles north of city. Hopeless. Sooooo sorry.**
>
> **Just now**

With a big smile on his face, he pressed the send button and logged off.

***

That afternoon, he checked Chad's Facebook frequently. Around 4:00 p.m., Billie sent him a private message requesting a private Facebook chat at 7:30 p.m. Although her request puzzled him, he immediately accepted.

***

At 7:30 sharp, Zach logged onto Chad's Facebook. Billie had already started the private chat session.

> **Billie P.**
> **I am so bummed out**
>
> **7:27 p.m.**

Chad
**Me 2. Was looking forward 2 our date. Of all the days,
she had 2 fall today.**

7:34 p.m.

Billie P.
can ur dad drive u

7:36 p.m.

Zach sighed loudly.

Where does she come up with all these ideas? he thought. *Why can't
she keep things simple? His mom broke her arm. Accept it and shut up.*

He didn't have time to wallow in his irritation. He had to
come up with a quick answer.

"Aha," he said, snapping his fingers.

Chad
Dad in Afghanistan.

7:40 p.m.

Billie P.
does he look like u?

7:42 p.m.

"What does this have to do with anything?" hissed Zach.

Chad
Sort of.

7:43 p.m.

Billie P.
**send me a picture of him in uniform @moms work they
have a huge bulletin board 4 photos of vets**

7:45 p.m.

"Oh brother," whispered Zach.

Chad

My dad is kind of weird. Doesn't like 2 be photographed.

7:48 p.m.

Billie P.
OMG I have a cousin like that
I always thought cuz she's like soooo ugly I'm sure will need tons of money 2 fix her messed up face not a problem 4 me maybe will b a model 1 day.

7:52 p.m.

Chad
Sure

7:54 p.m.

Billie P.
why don't I come 2 ur house?

7:56 p.m.

Dang, he thought. *Why can't she accept that I'm unable to come?*

Chad
Bad idea.

7:59 p.m.

Billie P.
It seem like u don't want 2 meet me

8:00 p.m.

Exactly, he thought.

Chad
I'm like dying 2 meet u, but u can't run 2 the house of somebody u met online. U need 2 meet them in a safe public place first. This is basic Internet safety. Suppose I'm not the person I claim 2 be?

8:06 p.m.

Billie P.

ooh shut up of course u r chad

8:07 p.m.

Chad
What makes u so sure?

8:08 p.m.

Billie P.
know it inside my heart

8:09 p.m.

Chad
So, u r going on a hunch. Hunches and online safety don't go together. No, no, no, I can't let u take all that risk.

8:12 p.m.

Billie P.
Ooh u r soooo sweet u r worried about my safety?

8:14 p.m.

Chad
Cuz I love u.

8:15 p.m.

Billie P.
how can we meet then

8:17 p.m.

Chad
Listen, school will be over in about 4 weeks. Mom will be able 2 drive me by then, and we can see each other as much as u want.

8:20 p.m.

Billie P.
Yes every day. 4 now we talk on the phone want 2 hear ur voice

8:22 p.m.

"Here she goes again," whispered Zach. "But, I seem to be

on a roll, and I'm sure I'll beat her."

Chad
Not a good idea.

8:25 p.m.

Billie P.
Why not? its safe.

8:26 p.m.

Chad
It'll spoil the surprise.

8:28 p.m.

Billie P.
don't get it

8:29 p.m.

Chad
When summer vacation starts, u'll see and hear me all at the same time. After weeks of anticipation, imagine the happiness and excitement when everything happens all at once.

8:35 p.m.

Billie P.
OMG sounds like a romance novel

8:37 p.m.

Zach exhaled as he resumed reading.

Billie P.
have a great idea we r members at the Green Valley neighborhood pool can bring a guest how about we meet there

8:38 p.m.

Chad
Great idea. Love both u and swimming.

8:39 p.m.

Billie P.
me 2

8:40 p.m.

Chad
And I love surprises after weeks of anticipation.

8:41 p.m.

Billie P.
OMG like the mother of all surprises

8:42 p.m.

Zach snickered.

Chad
u bet. When the time gets close, we can agree on the details.

8:44 p.m.

As Zach pressed the send button, he whispered, "That's when you'll be a pile of shredded fluff with a crushed heart."

Billie P.
OMG OMG soooooooooooooo excited ☺ B4N

8:45 p.m.

Chad
B4N

8:46 p.m.

Zach logged off with one hand as he wiped his sweaty forehead with the other. His plan was working better than expected.

CHAPTER 11

Sunday, May 15

After church and lunch at a nearby diner, Zach discovered Billie had publicized on Facebook their decision to delay their first date as soon as their chat was over.

> **Billie P.**
> chad and me will not talk or see each other till the first day of summer break we will meet at our neighborhood green valley pool
> Yearning and anticipation before the first date is the in thing in love our first date will b the bomb cuz we will dream about it 4 soooo long like he is the knight in shining armor and like I'm the fair maiden in a medieval romance novel
> dying 4 summer 2 start
> ooh chad my dearest knight no more private messages until it's time 2 work out the details of our pool date. Please forgive me 4 doing this I want 2 do the yearning and anticipation to the max before we meet ☺ ☺ ☺
> **16 hours ago**

Thank goodness, thought Zach when he read her message. This would make his life much simpler. Trying to be three different people at the same time was exhausting. Sometimes Zach had to focus very hard to figure out which person he was supposed to be at a given moment.

The replies from her friends were mostly positive. Her ability to be patient surprised some, while the idea of medieval love enchanted others. Some admitted being able to wait four days, but not four weeks. Although nobody mentioned it, Zach was confident the kids who went to the same pool were dying to meet Chad or, at least, catch a glimpse of him. Knowing Billie, Zach was sure she revealed all these details about her first date with Chad to ensure the presence of the biggest audience possible. Little did she know, there would be a nightmare awaiting her.

When he went to Samson's Facebook, he found a private message.

Gem Bardel

I wanted 2 write yesterday, but I had Saturday detention cuz those baboons called teachers "R right" all the time.

On Friday, I was in a bad mood. The stupid, albino substitute wanted me 2 go up 2 the board and solve a math problem. I told him 2 buzz-off and find somebody else. He got mad and sent me 2 the counselor.

Thanx 4 wanting 2 know more about my bad luck. U R the only one I can talk 2 openly. U make my life more bearable.

About that boy, why R U so worried about him? Do U always jump 2 defend people?

Now, let's go back 2 my story. As the fifth-grade year continued, the kids got meaner. It was hell at home, hell at school, and I was ticked off with everything and everybody. One day during recess, this short classmate kept on pulling my ponytail and screaming, "Ding dong," before running away. I asked her 2 stop, but she didn't. The laughter of the other kids and her annoying hair pulling made me super angry. One karate move dropped her in the dirt like a limp old mop. She stood up and ran away. Nobody bothered me after that. That was what those mean Pine City kids needed, a good whipping. They never became my friends, but they sure gave me respect. When I started grade 6 at Mills Magnet Middle School, I reinvented myself. I acted, I dressed, and I looked tough. A big size and 4 years of karate lessons helped a lot. I also found a couple of tough friends.

When I'm not in detention, I never spend recess or eat lunch alone. I have Amanda and Keisha.

Amanda and Keisha R alright, but I always have 2 pretend a lot around them. Deep inside, I don't feel that close 2 them.

3 hours ago

It sounds like the story of my life, Zach thought, feeling a pang of pain. *Mean kids never leave me alone, but I'm too puny and don't know any karate moves.* But was that the solution? They stopped bugging Gem but turned away from her, leaving her with no friends, forcing her to reinvent herself and pretend to be somebody she wasn't. Her new friends were right for the reinvented Gem, not the real one. At least Zach's friends were right for him. They're a bunch of misfits, but they get along great.

Samson 112

Saturday detention, yuck! Substitute teachers, double yuck.

Happy 2 be helpful. Why do kids have 2 be mean and pick on other kids? I wish school was a nicer place where everybody was accepted, and all the kids were friendly. Bullies always attack in places where the teacher on playground duty can't see them. That mean girl got what she deserved.

Going back 2 the boy, appearances can be deceiving. Maybe he was exchanging notes with ur archenemy or maybe he was passing them 2 somebody else. It's hard 4 a skinny little boy 2 say no 2 anybody. If I were u, I'd make sure exactly what was going on before doing anything.

Just now

Monday, May 16

Billie P.

adopted a 5 month old puppy from shelter puppy has long white hair with brown patches

OMG her hair so super frizzy I had to use a leave in anti-frizz conditioner after bath Tomorrow will start puppy school she's making messes everywhere.

Imagine my mom want me 2 clean up the messes OK mom I'm making it public I Billie Preston do not clean yucky messes so until she's potty trained its ur job!!!!!!!!!!!!

guess what I named her? Fafi click on the link and meet Fafi.

37 minutes ago

Zach clicked on the link where he saw a big fuzz ball of white and brown with droopy ears and a pointy face.

What an ugly puppy, he thought, but, of course, Chad had a different opinion.

Chad
What a cutie.
I stand behind u 100%. No kid should clean dog messes. Kids should only have fun.

Just now

Billie sent some more photographs of Fafi over the next few days without any comments.

Tuesday, May 17

As Mr. Doodash took roll, rain poured out from the dense, gray clouds that had threatened rain since last night. Following an indoor stretching routine, the teacher retrieved balls from a closet for the kids to shoot hoops on the basketball court. The balls, however, were not inflated to his satisfaction, so Mr. Doodash asked Jack to get the air pump and inflate them. He instructed the rest of the class to march in place. Zach was grateful for the rain because it made gym class manageable. However, an unexpected knock on the door ruined the rest of his day.

The assistant principal walked into the room, whispered something in the teacher's ear, and the two men quickly left the room. Mr. Doodash did not give his students any instructions before his departure. The students continued marching in place. Minutes passed. Mr. Doodash did not return. Gradually, some students slowed down to a standstill, some tossed the balls around or shot hoops, while others milled around aimlessly, trying to figure out what to do. Zach daydreamed about lunch as he marched in place.

Without catching Zach's attention, Billie, holding the air pump, appeared next to him.

"Let's inflate this scrawny boy," she squealed, poking him in the thigh with the pump's tip.

Startled, he pulled away and cried, "Leave me alone."

"You'll look much better when you fill up."

Zach, his shoulders hunched, hurried away crying, "Go away. Leave me alone."

It did not take long for the laughing to start. Clearly enjoying herself, Billie followed him, poking his back as she pumped air, her laughter intensifying with every poke.

"You'll have a buff body once I'm done inflating you," she said, cackling, her eyes twinkling with mischievous delight. "I promise."

"Go away. Leave me alone. Leave me alone," Zach continued to yell, wishing he could bust out of the ever-shrinking gymnasium and get rid of her and the nasty spectators.

The chase went on until somebody screamed, "He's back, he's back." Billie ran and shoved the pump into the closet.

When Mr. Doodash walked into the gym, the students were busy shooting hoops or marching in place as if nothing had happened. Stunned and on the verge of tears, Zach was the only idle one. Luckily, the teacher did not notice him, and he escaped an angry lecture.

Wednesday, May 18

Gem sent Samson a private message in the late afternoon.

Gem Bardel

On Monday, we figured out Victoria's locker combination. Yesterday afternoon, after the kids left school 2 catch their buses and rides, we invaded her locker. It was gross. Candy wrappers and crap everywhere! There was even a moldy piece of a mystery food. We tore the picture of her boyfriend that was taped 2 the inside of the door, broke the small mirror above it, tore some pages out of her math book, then dumped out all the crap from her pencil case on the floor. We did a lot of damage super-fast. Staying longer 2 trash a total dumpster wasn't worth the risk of being caught. Students doing after-school activities and some teachers were still in the building. Amanda's sister was waiting 4 us in her car outside the school. We hung out at Amanda's then me and Keisha rode the city bus

home. Cuz we knew we were going 2 be among the suspects, we agreed on one fib. When the principal met with us separately today, we all told her the same story (we went straight 2 Amanda's house after school where we hung out with her sister and baked brownies). Awesome! Well, we had planned the whole thing very carefully.

Victoria and her homies R super angry, but can't figure out who did it. Most awesome day ever!

About 1 hour ago

Gem's fate is now in my hands, thought Zach. *I know the secret that could ruin her in two minutes.*

CHAPTER 12

The raid of Victoria's locker was perhaps the biggest act of destruction in the school's history. It threw the whole school into hysteria after the cafeteria lady, the first person to enter the school, discovered the mess as she walked down the south hall on her way to the kitchen.

Victoria and Trish were passing notes like crazy. The principal, assistant principals, counselors, teachers, and students wanted to know who did it. The students gossiped about it insatiably, generating all kinds of rumors and speculations. Victoria had many enemies. Many names floated around, including Gem's.

I'm pretty sure Gem and her friends will get expelled for what they did, thought a victorious Zach. *Tomorrow, I'll rat on them to the counselor.*

He pulled his grammar booklet out of his backpack. As he worked on his homework, an unsettled feeling forced him to stop. He gazed at the white wall behind his bed.

What am I going to tell the counselor? he thought. *The school must be 100% sure before they expel anybody. I can't claim I saw them. On Tuesday, I left two hours early to go to the dentist. If I want her expelled, the counselor must see the message. The whole Samson game will get exposed, and I'll be in deep trouble with the school and my parents. The Nag-a-Lot will ground me forever. No, that would be stupid and dangerous. I must figure out something else.*

Victoria doesn't need all these strong proofs before an outright war between them starts. Zach could tell Victoria he overheard two eighth graders say they saw three girls who looked like Gem and her friends hurrying out of the south hall on Tuesday afternoon after most of the students were gone. Nope, bad idea. Victoria is a blabbermouth. No matter how much she'll promise to keep his name out, it'll slip out, getting Zach in trouble with Gem. Maybe tomorrow he could start a rumor. He could casually mention during lunch what he supposedly overheard the eighth graders talking about. In a couple of days, the kids would forget the rumor's originator and would change the details of the story a lot, but they would keep Gem at the center of the event. Although not as impressive as getting her expelled, starting a big war between Victoria and Gem is plenty good and good enough.

That was the moment Zach had been waiting for, but somehow he was unhappy. A feeling of emptiness gripped him as if a gaping hole had settled within him, rendering his triumph hollow. Throughout the evening, his discomfort made him restless and fidgety. The ever-shrinking house constricted him. He moved from room to room, in and out of the house, unable to settle anywhere for more than a few minutes. The image of a fluid monster chasing him awoke him several times, from his restless sleep, drenched in sweat.

Thursday, May 19

During the seventh-grade lunch period, the cafeteria was the usual scene. Each group of students occupied their regular tables. Victoria and her gang sat at one end while Gem and her gang sat at the opposite end. Posturing and knuckle-cracking were common actions whenever those two groups looked at each other. The popular girls, including Billie and the cheerleaders, occupied one large table, one table away from the football players. The other boy athletes occupied several tables close to the football players and across from the girl athletes' tables. Absorbed in their nerdy discussions, the geeks sat near the door. Everybody else was scattered around in small groups. The rejects like Zach and his friends gathered in small groups near the corners. Zach, Logan, and Isaac, who was a child of Malaysian immigrants, were terrible at sports, reasonably smart but not on a par with the nerds.

They sat in their usual arrangement; Zach and Isaac facing Logan, who sat with his back turned to the rest of the tables. When Logan brought his tray, their lunch started. Zach unwrapped his turkey sandwich and took a large bite that matched his hunger. As he chewed one bite after another, his eyes moved back and forth between Gem's table and Victoria's table. The strong negative vibes Zach sensed between the two groups made him wonder whether Victoria had figured out who invaded her locker. Probably not. Otherwise, Logan, the king of gossip, would have delivered the news before even setting his tray on the table. Zach, however, knew Gem was on Victoria's list of suspects. With no evidence and many other enemies, Victoria was not likely to act.

"Look at Billie and her friends cracking up," said Isaac. "I saw her looking at us just before they laughed."

"I bet they're laughing at us," said Logan, sounding annoyed.

"A day will come when she'll pay the price," said Zach calmly, the memory of the air pump chase still fresh in his mind. "Don't worry."

"Oh, wow," said Isaac.

"Now, you're making prophecies," said Logan, raising one eyebrow.

Caught off guard, Zach wondered if he had said too much, or if he would be suspected when he delivered his final blow?

"Ah, she's not worth it," said Isaac.

"Guess what?" said Logan with a chuckle, "During Miss Atherton's pizza party, that big freckled eighth grader got into a food fight with three other boys. They all had to stay after school and clean the bathrooms."

To Zach's relief, Billie seemed a million miles away from his friends' minds. The conversation took many turns, covering a wide range of topics, including Victoria's locker. Lunch finished without Zach attempting to start his intended rumor about Gem's attack on Victoria's locker. He wasn't sure why he didn't follow through with his plan. Perhaps he was afraid he would do it wrong, and his name would somehow get mentioned. Then he'd be in real trouble, especially if Gem still believed he was Victoria's spy. Perhaps he needed more time to refine his strategy.

Friday, May 20

Another school day passed. Zach did not utter a single word regarding the attack on Victoria's locker. Despite his determination, something inside him prevented him from linking Gem to the incident even in the most casual way. No moment felt right to start a rumor. For a passing moment, it seemed downright wrong to harm somebody who had suffered in so many ways. But what about *his* pain? During that instant, it all felt trivial, almost irrelevant.

Saturday, May 21

Billie posted a message on her wall.

> **Billie P.**
> **Yeah I'm remodeling my room**
> **pink walls are so yesterday my new color is soooo today stay tuned 4 the next message 2 find out new color**
>
> **now have 2 sleep on couch for 2 nights yuck** ☹
> **5 hours ago**

What an oppressed little creature, Zach thought, rolling his eyes.

"How am I going to respond to this bratty stupidity?" he said to himself.

He was tempted not to respond, but sensitive Chad needed to sympathize with his girlfriend's miseries.

> **Chad**
> **Poor Billie. My heart goes out 2 u.**
> **Just now**

No, the sarcasm is too obvious, he thought.

He deleted the message and restarted.

> **Chad**
> **Can't wait 2 know the new color of ur room.**
> **Hang in there 4 the 2 nights. Sleeping on the couch sucks, but getting a remodeled room is worth it.**
> **Just now**

Satisfied with his message, he clicked on send.

Sunday, May 22

Zach found a private message from Gem on Samson's Facebook page.

> **Gem Bardel**
> **Halloween in 6th grade was a big trick. We lost our**

house. My parents stopped paying the mortgage three months after the accident. The bank took back the house and sold it at an auction. We had 2 live 4 weeks in a house where all the neighbors read the sign about the upcoming auction every time they passed by.

Now we live in a 2-story rental condo in the industrial part of the city near the railroad tracks, a rough neighborhood. Here being tough is a big plus. During the day, it is OK, but after dark it is scary. There R shootouts. We don't leave the condo after dark.

The new place has 2 bedrooms and only 1 bathroom on the second floor. The 4 of us bunk in 1 room and fight all the time. The ground floor is one open room, with a kitchen in one corner and the rest is a living/dining area. Our condo is tight and uncomfortable. Every couple of weeks, something breaks down—the toilet, the water heater, the furnace, the fridge, or whatever. The window ACs growl but barely work. It is cheaper and less irritating 2 keep them off. During heat waves, they take the edge off the heat, making the condo more bearable, but never real cool.

The backyard is tiny. It seems barely enough 4 a hamster 2 play in. Ginger was miserable. On days when my dad wasn't totally depressed, he took her out 4 a walk. The sight of the car shops reminded him of his bad hand, putting him back in a bad mood 4 days. On the weekends, me or 1 of my brothers walked her. One day, my parents decided they couldn't afford 2 feed Ginger and take her 2 the vet anymore. She was 2 expensive. My mom went 2 a nice neighborhood with big yards and posted ads everywhere. A nice old lady adopted Ginger early in the summer. I cried the day my mom put her in the car and took her 2 the woman's house. We all wanted 2 go there, but all our begging and pleading didn't change her mind. She thought the presence of children would complicate things. My dad sat on the couch like a lump, teary-eyed and gloomy. I was upset 4 weeks, even though I knew it was in Ginger's best interest, seeing how unhappy she was in our so-called yard. Oh, how much I miss Ginger. How much I miss my life in Minnesota.

I wish the police would find the person who caused all

our miseries and make him pay. I hope he rots in hell. Sometimes I feel like exploding from frustration and anger.

By the way, U were right about the boy. After we trashed Victoria's locker, Keisha saw him passing notes between Victoria and her friend Trish without even glancing at them. U should see Victoria. She's very scary, and a scrawny, little boy wouldn't dare say no 2 her. Keisha remembered it was the teacher who put him between Victoria and Trish 2 keep them from talking and disrupting the class with their blabbering.

I ruffled him real bad when he didn't really do anything bad. That morning, we had no hot water, and the toilet was clogged. I felt mean.

U know, I've been a little calmer since I met U. U have made my life a bit more bearable.

3 hours ago

Gem's last statement pleased Zach. He never knew that a rejected nobody like him could have such a good impact on anybody's life. Reflecting on Gem's behavior since she opened up to Samson, he realized that although Gem was still rough, she had been in fewer fights. A part of him was relieved he hadn't mentioned anything about the locker incident as she had been hurt in more ways than he had imagined. The other part of him still held a grudge, insisting on starting a war between her and Victoria. She needed to pay for snatching his ball and ice cream bar, and for beating him up for no reason. The broken water heater and clogged toilet were not his fault or problem. Samson, of course, had to show her lots of support and sympathy.

Samson 112
Don't blame u 4 being frustrated and angry. Not sure why some people have 2 suffer so much while others have it easy. Sooooo unfair.
Glad I can give u some help. Wish I could do more.

Just now

In Facebook land, Samson and Chad lived in two different worlds; a world of anger and frustration and a world of fuzzy bunnies and colorful bonbons. Zach felt squashed between the two.

CHAPTER 13

Wednesday, May 25

In the afternoon, Billie posted a message on her wall.

> **Billie P.**
> **please join me on a tour of a bedroom fit 4 a girl starting her teens.**
>
> **4 hours ago**

I turned thirteen months ago, thought Zach. *It was just another birthday. I don't understand what the big deal is.*

He clicked on the YouTube link. A spot the color of egg yolk appeared on the screen. As the camera zoomed out, the spot turned into a wall.

"Tah dah," said Billie, standing a few feet away from the wall, her hand pointing to it. "Sunny-yellow rocks."

The camera moved swiftly from one wall to the next, focusing on the framed photos of Michael Jackson and Lady Gaga, the pale yellow closet doors, and the bright-yellow curtains with scattered deep-purple smiley faces. In the corner next to the window, a green dog bed monogrammed "FAFI" laid on the yellow carpet.

"This is Fafi's bed," said Billie, as if it wasn't obvious, without appearing on the screen. "She'll move into it when she graduates from puppy school. Now, she stays in the backyard."

The room turned upside-down and then swirled as the camera moved swiftly in a shaky hand, probably that of her younger brother, before stopping and focusing upside-down, then right-side-up on a huge bed, covered with a green comforter and what seemed like a million pillows and cushions in different shades of green.

Zach wondered if there was enough space on the bed for

Billie to sleep.

"A bed fit for a princess," gloated Billie, still without appearing on the screen.

"A crazy one," whispered Zach.

In the usual style, the camera swiftly moved until it focused on a small green table with an arched mirror. A blow-dryer, a variety of curling irons, a couple of hair brushes, and an assortment of small jars, and other make-up items, similar to things Zach had seen in his mother's room, cluttered the table.

"My dressing table," said Billie, standing next to the table and fidgeting with the clutter. "Looking pretty is hard work, but it is a lot of fun at the same time. I love my new room, walls like the sun and furniture like the fields in the spring."

Billie walked over to the window and pulled the curtains open.

In a voice reminiscent of that of a circus host, she said, "I hope you enjoyed the tour. Bye-bye for now."

Her room is as wacky as her, thought Zach.

Chad's reply came as swift as the camera's movements in the hand of Billie's little brother.

Chad
What a beautiful room! The design is revolutionary and radical. The concept of the yellow sun and green fields is smoking hot.

Just now

The responses were mostly flattering although a few insisted pink was the true girly color.

Sunday, May 29

In the afternoon, Billie posted a message on her wall.

Billie P.
happy birthday 2 me today I officially turn 13
finished the festivities with family/friends with lunch at my favorite place Fluffy's Tacos. OMG how much I love their tacos.

last night my dad treated me and five of my bestest best friends Jill Hannah Lizzie Emma and Kim 2 a fancy French restaurant la poule doree a super funny place!!! imagine chicken fried steak is called escalope and flan is called cream caramel LOL

after that dad drove us 2 mom's house where we had a slumber party in my new room stayed up till 3 and had a blast

click on the link and have a sneak peek at our fun party

PS: THKs Hannah 4 shooting the video and missing being in this fun video

52 minutes ago

Zach clicked on the link.

Five girls wearing frilly pajamas, squealing and laughing hysterically, jumped on the bed as they displayed their fingernails, each painted a different color, black, green, yellow, blue, orange, red, purple, pink, gold, and silver. Billie's pajamas were white, while those of her friends were purple.

The video lasted a little over two minutes. Towards the end, Zach felt like exploding from boredom and irritation.

Of course, what seemed like an endless number of happy birthday messages from her friends filled her Facebook page. Who dared forget about her birthday? They would undoubtedly face the dreadful consequences of isolation and humiliation. Having wasted enough time on Billie's message and video, he skimmed rapidly through the messages. Despite Zach's annoyance, he felt obligated to send her two messages: one as Chad, of course, and one as himself to avoid cruel remarks in the school's hallways; he was already receiving enough of those.

Chad

Happy birthday 2 the most wonderful 13 year old in the whole wide world. Enjoyed watching the video a lot. By the way, u looked very cute in ur white pajamas.

Just now

He waited for another hour or so before sending a message from himself.

Zach Higgins
Have a very happy birthday. FUN sleepover!

Just now

Enough of that, he thought as he logged off. *Let silly Billie finish her celebrations before I deliver the final blow. D-Day is tomorrow when she'll know the taste of real pain—that taste I know so well.*

CHAPTER 14

Monday, May 30 (Memorial Day)

After two weeks of medieval lovers' anticipation and a variety of birthday treats, Zach was ready for the final blow. He sent Billie a private message Monday afternoon.

> **Chad**
> **We went on our yearly Memorial Day picnic. Some NASTY dog bit me. Does not look good.**
>
> **Just now**

***

Over a week had passed without receiving any private messages from Gem. She had not even participated in any of the wrestling discussions with her friends or commented on any of his wrestling links, something she had always done. Worry crept into Zach's heart.

At bedtime, he checked Samson's Facebook page for the fifth time and Chad's for the first. There were no messages. Zach did not know why, but Gem's disappearance from the web bothered him and put him in a state of turmoil. On the other hand, Billie's absence barely disturbed him. He always knew Billie would respond soon enough.

Tuesday, May 31

When Zach saw Billie in the cafeteria, she seemed kind of pale, but he wasn't sure if he was imagining things. His friends did not mention Billie, and he decided not mention her either.

At home, he first checked Samson's Facebook page, hoping

to find something from Gem, but there was nothing. Chad, on the other hand, had a private message.

Billie P.
u poor thing r u in a lot of pain? where did it bite u? did ur looks get messed up? don't worry mom knows a great plastic surgeon.

8 hours ago

"And at school she calls *me* dummy," snapped Zach, rolling his eyes. "*She* is the dummy. I say it doesn't look good, and she tells me about a plastic surgeon."

Chad
OMG. It's real bad. I have rabies, the real bad kind. Have about 72 hours to live. Doctor ordered my family 2 lock me in my room 4 their own protection. They slide my food under the door, and we talk by phone. Pain is horrible. I'm suffering and dying slow and painful. Love u and feel so bad about dying and leaving u, my soul mate, behind.

Just now

How about that, Billie? Zach thought as a wicked smile lit up his face.

Just before hitting the send button, a naughty thought crossed his mind. Wouldn't it be more fun if Billie witnessed Chad's agonizing death over the phone? He would get to hear her cry her devastated heart out over the loss of her wonderful, handsome Chad. His friend Patrick was in drama club. He would make a perfect dying Chad. Wouldn't this be much more dangerous? Ah, what the heck. She didn't know Patrick's phone number and he'd choose a time when Patrick's parents were still at work. Knowing Patrick's sense of humor, Zach knew he'd love the whole game. Zach added to his message Patrick's home number and asked Billie to call on Thursday at 4:00 p.m. When he hit the send button, a wider and wickeder smile lit up his face.

CHAPTER 15

After dinner, Zach finally found a private message from Gem.

Gem Bardel
WE HAVE MOVED AGAIN!
My parents couldn't even afford 2 keep the dumpy duplex. As usual, we didn't know about the move until the last minute. Now we R living with Grandma Cordelia in her teeny, tiny 2 bedroom apartment at the Tuscan Deluxe Apartments. Believe me, there is nothing deluxe about these apartments. At least it's in a little better neighborhood, the burger joint where my mom works is in the nearby strip mall, and the bus stop is in front of the building.

My parents and little sister R sharing the extra bedroom, the boys R sleeping on the couches in the living room, and I'm sleeping on a rollaway bed in the kitchen. Grandma wakes up very early and heads straight 2 the kitchen, rolling her squeaky oxygen tank carrier. She moans and groans loudly from the pain in her joints, and generates so much noise while brewing her coffee, it's impossible 2 stay asleep, but I pretend 2 be asleep cuz she needed some convincing before allowing us 2 move in with her. I'm so scared we'll end up on the street. Every day at least one person visits the kitchen in the middle of the night 4 a drink of water or whatever.

As usual, my dad either barricades himself in his room or watches TV in the living room. Interacting with him is frustrating. His moodiness drives everybody crazy. In one instant, he can flip from sarcastic 2 bitter, 2 playful, 2 wicked, 2 silly.

We've been in this house 4 only 6 days and I feel I'm suffocating. By the way, we sold our computer for 50 bucks because we needed the money. It took me a while 2 discover the small public library five blocks away from Grandma's house where I'm now writing this message. At least I still can communicate with U. Although U write very little, U have such a soothing effect. I don't know what I would have done without U.

23 minutes ago

After reading this latest chapter on Gem's miseries, whatever grudge a small part of him still held against her dissipated. She had plenty of hardships to deal with and didn't need more. Funny how that whole Facebook thing started to get back at her for beating him up, then somehow the correspondence calmed her down enough to get her into less trouble and to think before jumping to conclusions. After all, the scrawny boy wasn't a spy, but a victim of bad luck. Maybe all Gem needed was a friend to whom she could talk frankly and freely without any pretenses. Maybe bullying was a crazy and sick way to offload her anger and frustrations.

Samson 112
Soooooooooo very sorry. No one person deserves that. I wish I could help u more, but I'm just a kid.

Just now

After sending the message to Gem, he went to Chad's Facebook page, where he found a private message.

Billie P.
OMG can't believe it all the anticipation and the summer plans ruined u'll be gone forever
been crying since I read ur message I'll call u thursday at 4:00 sharp.

About 1 hour ago

The plan was working as intended.

Wednesday, June 1

Billie looked a mess. Her long, sleek hair was put up in a messy knot.

Her eyes were bloodshot, and eyelids were puffy. Kids noticed Billie's appearance, but nobody knew what was wrong with her because she mentioned nothing about Chad dying from rabies on her Facebook page or in school. The grapevines were full of speculations; the most common ones were that Billie was grounded or ill. Zach was on top of the world and had to work very hard to keep his elation from showing.

Billie's silence did not surprise Zach. Billie broadcasted what she thought was worth bragging about. Everything else she buried deep inside herself. Only good and exciting things happened to Billie. That's what she wanted the whole wide world to believe. Zach also was sure Billie wouldn't allow Chad to leave her Facebook world as a result of dying from rabies. Chad would exit her cyber world whenever she chose and after she devised a creative, positive spin on his departure.

Later that day, there was a private message from Gem.

Gem Bardel

U don't have 2 do more of anything. Your presence is enough. If only Dad's right hand worked, then everything would be different.

I have in-school detention 4 the rest of the year, i.e. 7 days, 4 being too mouthy with the geography teacher. She was talking about her boring mountains and valleys. I started doodling. She took my doodles away and asked me 2 pay attention. I tried but got bored, so I doodled again. She yelled at me and asked me 2 pay attention. I yelled back and told her 2 shut up and mind her own business. Off I went 2 the counselor's office.

Do U have in-school detention in New York? If U don't, then let me explain it 2 U. Well, U go 2 school every day, but instead of going 2 your classes, U go 2 some room where U have to do all your class work, eat lunch, and spend your recess. So dumb!

2 hours ago

No wonder he didn't see her in the cafeteria during lunch.

Samson 112

Yuck. BORING. Hang in there. School will be over in days. At least u won't have 2 deal with the annoying teachers.

Soooooo sorry about ur dad. If only his right hand worked. If only. What a bummer.

Just now

Thursday, June 2

Billie was absent. Wow, that was more success than Zach had anticipated. A little suffering was good medicine for a selfish brat like her. She had made him suffer so much and for too long. That's what he called brilliant conniving—a well-developed plan executed with patience and precision. Delighted, proud, and victorious, he moved around the school pretending to be totally oblivious to anything Billie-related.

When the threesome sat together as usual for lunch, Logan said, as he put his tray down on the table, "I was right. Billie was a mess yesterday because she was coming down with something. She's absent today."

"Really?" declared Zach, his eyes widening with surprise. "I didn't notice."

"Since when did you notice anything?" Isaac remarked.

The three laughed.

***

After school, Zach rode his bicycle, peddling as if a monster was chasing him, the two blocks separating his house from Patrick's.

His jolly, redheaded friend didn't look his usual self when he opened the door. A wave of dread swept over Zach. He wondered if Patrick had changed his mind about playing Chad. He had seemed very excited about the whole thing when they discussed it the day before. Zach's impulse was to ask Patrick whether the game was still on, but he decided against it. Instead, he walked into the living room, sat on the couch, and turned on the TV. Patrick sat next to him.

"My mom is home," Patrick whispered, a hint of alarm in his voice.

Taken aback, Zach felt tongue-tied.

"Isn't she supposed to leave work at five?" he finally asked.

"Yes, but she left early because she didn't feel well."

Patrick always complained about how late his mother worked. Zach could not believe his bad luck. Of all the days in the year, she had to come early today. But, no matter how bad the situation was, he had to work around it, and his plan had to succeed.

"Where's she now?" he asked as he tried to formulate a new strategy.

"In her room."

"Is she asleep?"

"Maybe."

"I'll tell you what, let's take the phone off the charger and keep it close to us. As soon as it rings, we'll grab it and run to the back porch."

Nodding in agreement, Patrick grinned, then obediently brought the cordless phone and placed it on the coffee table in front of them.

With great diligence, Zach kept an eye on the digital clock hanging on the wall above the TV. The minutes crawled: 3:39, 3:40, 3:41… His excitement intensified with the passage of every minute. At 3:55, he heard shuffling down the hall.

"What's that?" he asked, alarmed.

"Mom," said Patrick, sounding equally alarmed.

"We need her out of this area quickly."

"Maybe she'll refill her glass of water and go back to her room. She did that just before you came. Just act normal, and pretend to be watching the show."

From the corner of his eye, Zach saw Patrick's mom, a glass in her hand, enter the kitchen. Then, he heard the whoosh of the water coming out of the faucet before stopping abruptly. As she shuffled back to her room, she suddenly stopped and peeked into the living room.

"Zach," she said, "I haven't seen you in a while."

"I've been around," he answered in a detached tone, keeping his eyes fixed on the TV to give the impression of being absorbed in the show.

"You guys seem to like this show. I won't distract y…Oh, oh, what's the phone doing over there? Patrick, how many times have I told you to always keep it charging?"

She walked into the room, grabbed the phone with her free

hand, then headed out. When Zach opened his mouth to complain, Patrick gave him a nudge and whispered to shush. Realizing how close four o'clock was, Zach went along. The main thing was for her to return quickly to her room. When she started to shuffle down the hall in the direction of her room, Zach exhaled. As soon as she's out of the hall, he planned to bring the phone back. A commercial came on. She reversed her direction and returned to the living room.

"Did your mom find a roofer?"

Zach glanced at the clock. It was 3:57. *Yikes,* he thought. *Why now?*

"Don't know," he said, shrugging his shoulders.

"The roofer who did my boss's roof is great. If she hasn't found one, she should check him out."

"Cool."

He started going through the channels while humming a tune, signaling his desire to end the conversation.

"I'll call her later tonight," she said. "First I need to find his card. I believe I put it in the little basket next to the phone."

CHAPTER 16

Zach's eyes opened wide, his sweat glands on overdrive. It was 3:58. She had to leave.

In a flash he was standing next to her, Patrick at his heels.

"Your health is now the most important thing, Mrs. O'Brian," he said in a concerned tone. "You need to go back to bed."

"Thanks for your concern, but I feel much better."

"You're ill and could get worse quickly if you don't go back to bed," said Zach emphatically, trying to imitate his mother.

"Darn, I can't find anything in this cluttered doohickey. One of these days, I'll get organized."

"I'm sure you'll find the card easily after you rest in bed," said Zach.

"Zach is right, Mom. Why don't you go to bed and let me look for the card?"

Mrs. O'Brian gave the two boys a long, mysterious look.

"I thought you were watching TV. Why all this sudden interest in my health?"

"I'm the son of a nurse. I can't help it."

"And I love you," Patrick chimed in.

"Here, it is."

A wave of relief swept over Zach. *Now she'll go back to her room,* he thought.

"Red Bird Plumbing. Shoot. I'm sure it's here somewhere," she said, resuming her search.

Horror replaced the relief Zach had felt a few seconds before.

The microwave clock read 4:01. The phone rang. Zach shivered. In a desperate attempt, he reached around Mrs. O'Brian and grabbed the cordless phone.

"What do you think you're doing?" she asked harshly.

The phone rang for the second time.

"It's for us," Zach said as he scurried away.

Mrs. O'Brian ran after him. The phone rang for the third time. In a surprising move, she snatched the phone and pressed the answer button.

"Hello," she said.

Paralyzed by the fear of what was to come, Zach stopped and gazed at Mrs. O'Brian, his face the color of a corpse. Patrick stood behind him as if seeking protection. Weeks of careful planning and precise execution evaporated in a fraction of a second. His meticulously woven scheme tumbled over his head as if struck by the strongest earthquake in history.

"Who's already dead?" asked Mrs. O'Brian.

It was all unraveling. In his helpless devastation, Zach wished he'd evaporate or the earth would swallow him or the phone lines would get all tangled up or Billie would suddenly lose her voice forever. So many possibilities, but none was going to happen.

"There is no Chad here...Please, calm down and repeat what you said...Yes, that's the correct number...I'm sure nobody is dying from rabies, but I have a feeling a dead rat is starting to stink. Please tell me the story of Chad."

Thousands of minutes seemed to pass. Mrs. O'Brian listened to Billie, and said, "Aha" from time to time while shooting glares at the two boys that felt like poisonous darts.

"I need to figure out a couple of things first. Give me your number, sweetie, and I'll call you later tonight. I promise."

With the phone back on its base, Mrs. O'Brian looked straight at the boys, her eyes overflowing with suspicion.

"Who's Chad?"

Zach opened his eyes wide, pretending to be surprised and stretched his lips into a silly smile.

"Don't know any Chads," he said as innocently as he could muster.

"Country in Africa," said Patrick, his face turning beet-red.

"I said who not what," snapped his mom. "It's a person I'm talking about."

"It was probably a wrong number," said Zach.

"Nope," said Mrs. O'Brian, "it was a call for you. You snatched the phone from my hand and ran away with it for Pete's sake."

"We were expecting a call about an airsoft gun from a boy who was selling his cheap," Zach said. "Not that crazy person you talked to."

"There are druggies out there," said Patrick. "They imagine things and think they're real. Then they start calling around. We studied that in the anti-drug campaign at school."

"Really?" his mom said, giving him a piercing look. "There is something fishy going on. Zach, I want you to go home. I'll call your mom when she returns from work. Together, we'll get to the bottom of it all."

"We were going to play cards," said Zach, trying to delay his return home.

"Goodbye, Zach," Mrs. O'Brian said firmly.

Zach left their house, wondering how many years he'd be grounded.

CHAPTER 17

Zach's mom entered the house a little after 6:00 p.m. and threw her purse and keys on the counter. Zach, a big smile pasted on his face, ran to greet her.

"Good evening," he said cheerfully.

"Good evening. How was your day?"

"Wonderful. I finished all my homework, practiced my handwriting, and practiced the fiddle."

"That's the first bit of good news I've heard today," she said as a smile crept over her tired face. "My day was horrible from the accident clogging the highway this morning to everything going wrong at the hospital. At least the day will end on a good note."

Zach gulped, knowing that the happy note was only a temporary notion and dreading the moments, days, months, and perhaps years following the exposure of his convoluted fabrications.

"Where's dad?" she asked.

"He'll be working late tonight."

"Ah, well. It'll be the two of us eating dinner. I'm too tired to prepare anything. I'll heat a frozen pizza. We have blueberries for dessert."

"Yum. Blueberries, the super food."

"How wonderful! You now like what's good for you," she said, her face beaming. "You're definitely maturing."

"I'm almost thirteen and a half."

"Whoever said teenagers are difficult," she said, making a dismissive gesture with her hand.

As soon as she put the pizza in the oven, the phone rang. Zach's heart fell.

Zach's mom answered the phone, her back facing him. After the usual pleasantries, she listened for what seemed like a long time before saying, "Is that so?" This pattern persisted for a while. Zach felt hotter with every utterance his mom made. Throughout the conversation, she never turned around to look at him, making him more petrified as the minutes passed.

Once the conversation was over, she turned around and looked straight at him, her face deadly serious, her eyes blazing with anger.

"Mrs. O'Brian told me all about Billie," she said.

"Billie, who?" he said casually.

"Billie Preston," she said, raising her eyebrows, "the girl you've been going to school with since kindergarten."

"What's up with her?" he said smiling foolishly.

"Patrick confessed everything to his mom. Game over."

That weakling! thought Zach. *I shouldn't have trusted him.*

"Mrs. O'Brian called the poor girl back," proceeded Zach's mom. "She told her everything about the *dying Chad.*"

Zach lowered his head out of devastation over the catastrophic failure of his carefully designed plot rather than any feelings of remorse.

"Now, Zachariah Kermit, you need to call her and apologize!"

"Don't know her number."

His mom walked out of the room, returning shortly with the school directory in her hand.

"Problem solved," she said, sounding as if her patience was about to expire. "Stop coming up with excuses, and call her NOW."

"No way," he snapped as he stood up and started to walk out of the room.

"Zachariah Kermit," she yelled, "COME BACK NOW!"

Quickly he returned, mumbling his apologies.

"Do you realize how much devastation you caused this poor girl with your vicious plan? You invented this Chad, made her care about him, then you told her he was dying. You gave her so much heartache. She was weeping hysterically from all the distress when she spoke to Mrs. O'Brian. The least you can do is apologize for all the pain you caused her."

"What about the pain *she caused me* all these months?" he said, his eyes welling up with tears. "She treated me like a bug, insulting me all the time and in front of everybody. All I did was give her a little taste of her own medicine. Perhaps she'll learn something."

His mother's face softened, seeing the sincere pain on his face. She gently grabbed his chin and looked into his teary eyes.

"Why didn't you tell me?" she whispered. "I could have talked to the counselor and her mom. Her mom seemed like a reasonable and down-to-earth woman when we served on a PTA committee a few years ago. I'm sure we could have come up with some solution other than you going down to her level."

In frustration, he closed his eyes, allowing the captive tears to flow down his cheeks.

"Shorty, scrawny, midget, puny, stunted, dummy, clumsy," he recited whatever he could remember of Billie's insults. "She's a big, bad, mean bully."

"And what do you think you are now?" she said, reverting to a more serious tone.

He wiped his tears with the back of his hand, slowly opening his eyes, trying to wrap his mind around her suggestive question. Was he a bully? No way! He was just getting back at Billie for bullying him. He wasn't like Gem; a bullied person turned into a bully. But again, he didn't have Gem's size and four years of karate under his belt or Billie's popularity to let him get away with whatever punches or harsh words he threw around.

"What's this stench?" Mrs. Higgins said, walking around the kitchen, sniffing like a dog. Zach's congested nose barely detected anything.

"Oh, no, the pizza... I totally forgot about it."

She pulled out the smoking pizza, setting off the smoke alarm. Quickly, she doused the pizza with water and opened the window. Within seconds, the alarm stopped.

"There goes our dinner," she said with a sigh. "Perhaps for the better. It probably would have given me heartburn. Now where were we? Yes, the apology. Go ahead. Call her."

"If both of us are bullies, then we're even. No need to do anything."

"Back to the games. Call Billie or I will," she said firmly. "And put it on speaker phone."

CHAPTER 18

With trembling hands, he dialed the number.

"Hello," he said, responding to Billie's greeting, his voice barely audible.

"Who is it?"

"Zach," he said, trying to project his voice with little success.

"What do you want, stunted, mean monster?" she screamed.

"To apologize for the pain I caused you."

His mom nodded and smiled.

"What am I supposed to do with your apology? Clean the toilet?"

He wanted to tell her to ask Mrs. Melissa Jade Higgins, but instead, he followed his mother's whispered instructions.

"Can you please forgive me?"

"I'll make you pay for what you did, dwarf."

Zach swallowed hard. *She's going to shred me to pieces.*

"You think what you did to me was that small?" she continued. "Oh, no. I'm going to hold a grudge until forever, and I'm going to show you what a Billie grudge is."

Cold sweat ran down Zach's back. He was certain a Billie grudge would be nastiness ballooned into an ugly horror.

"Grudges will ruin your beauty," he said, not knowing how he came up with such a concept, probably from the depth of his horror. "They give people zits, warts, dark circles under their eyes, wrinkles, and all sorts of horrible things."

He glanced at his mother. A big question mark was written all over her face. Her eyes were wide, and her mouth hung slightly open.

"How do you know?" asked Billie, alarm detectable in her voice.

"My mom. She's a nurse."

A long silence followed before an agitated Billie said, "I don't know if I can erase what you did from my memory."

"Maybe you can try."

"Mrs. O'whatever—I can't remember her name—said her son told her you did that because I was mean to you. Me? Mean? What's up with that?"

Stunned by her lack of awareness, Zach gasped with shocked disbelief.

"What's up? I'll tell you what's up," he said, forgetting all his fears. "You called me names all the time. Short, puny, scrawny, and all sorts of names related to my size. You just called me stunted and dwarf a minute ago."

"I was telling the truth; that's all. The truth shouldn't upset anybody."

"In elementary school, you were more popular than most kids and ten thousand times more popular than me. But remember how mad you'd get when somebody mentioned anything about your weight? They w…"

"Shut up. Don't remind me of those days," she interrupted in her typical melodramatic fashion.

"They were telling the truth, too."

"What you did was mean and evil. You put this complicated plan together to make me fall in love with an invented guy, then you broke my heart when you said he was dying a painful death. All I did was say a few words for fun. Come on, don't you have any sense of humor?"

"I'm not popular like you to throw around mean words and get away with it. Anyway, amusing some kids by hurting the feelings of others is cruel. Just a quick reminder, in elementary school, I never ever made fun of your weight and was nice enough to give you my homemade banana muffins."

"I told you not to remind me of those days."

"Alright, alright. I just wanted to say that I don't care about how people look. What's important to me is what's on the inside."

"I always say beauty requires sacrifice," said Billie in a manner reminiscent of a commercial. "For the sake of my precious beauty, I won't carry a grudge. Besides, you're too pathetic and unimportant for ME, BILLIE, to waste my valuable time messing with you. Bye."

"Bye."

Zach put down the phone, satisfied with the results of the

conversation, but dreading the Nag-a-Lot's punishments—or consequences, as she liked to call them. He looked at his mother, his head full of questions.

"That went well," she said, sounding satisfied, a pale smile appearing on her face.

"Yes," he said, nodding his head in agreement, "for the sake of her precious beauty, she won't hold any grudges and won't mess with me anymore. What more can I ask for?"

"Nothing," said his mother. "This girl seems so insecure despite being quite popular," she added thoughtfully.

"No wonder she's so obsessed with looks—hers and everybody else's."

"And you managed to press the right button to get her off your back."

"I was so freaked out. I didn't know what in the world I was pressing."

"Deep inside your brain, you knew how much she's preoccupied with her beauty, so you identified the correct button."

"I guess," said Zach, feeling more relaxed, a gleam of hope creeping into his heart, promising leniency.

His mother shifted her weight from one leg to the other as the faint smile faded from her face and the intense anger returned to her eyes.

"But don't think it's over. There will be consequences for your dirty Facebook game. I'm not so sure what. I'm trying to figure it out. Some food will help recharge my brain. I haven't had anything to eat since this morning."

"I don't feel like eating," he said, all hopes of leniency dissipating. "I'll be in my room."

"You need your nourishment too. We still have a long night ahead of us."

Zach sighed, and sat at the kitchen table, suspense gnawing at him. His eyes darted around the room as if searching for an escape.

The dinner was peanut butter and jelly sandwiches and the dreaded, nasty blueberries.

She wolfed down her sandwich, while Zach nibbled on his. He wondered about the punishments she was formulating in her head as she chewed her food. Awkward silence hovered over them.

CHAPTER 19

After inhaling her sandwich, Zach's mother grabbed a handful of blueberries and stuffed them in her mouth. She placed the second handful on Zach's plate as he continued to nibble on the first half of his sandwich. She then emptied the rest of the blueberries into her palm and shoved them into her mouth. Seemingly unaware of the dribble of purple juice streaming down the side of her overstuffed mouth, she quickly cleared the table, only leaving behind Zach's plate. The clatter of plates and utensils placed carelessly in the sink made Zach cringe. Still holding the partially eaten half sandwich with one hand, he grabbed a blueberry with the other hand, and bit into it, wondering what terrible things she was devising.

With the same speed and noise level, his mother rinsed and loaded dishes into the dishwasher. Too nervous to swallow one more morsel, Zach emptied the contents of his plate into the trash then placed it quietly next to the sink. His mother grabbed the plate and put it in the dishwasher before slamming its door shut. The sweat ran down Zach's back.

"Well, what are the consequences?" asked Zach as soon as he summoned enough courage to speak, eager to get it over with.

"I have a pretty good idea what they'll be, but I'm still finalizing some points."

She wiped the table with a paper towel. Zach leaned against the sink, anxiously watching her.

"I want you to take me," she said as she walked away from the table, "to where that Chad lives or lived in cyber land. I want to see for myself all the correspondences between Billie and Chad or you, whatever."

Chills ran down Zach's spine, hearing her use her irritated-to-the-max voice. Dutifully, he led her to his room and went straight to Chad's Facebook page. They sat side by side. Pokerfaced, the face she put on so well when she wanted to torture anybody, she read all the messages in complete silence.

"What a sick movie," she said, when she finished reading, disgust dripping from her voice. "I can't believe I raised such a son. Now let's move on to your consequences."

Finally, thought Zach. He was ready to get it over with even if he was getting the death sentence. That would be better than all the dread.

"First, you will be participating in as many summer sports camps as I can find."

Zach cringed. She chose the thing he most hated. What a cruel punishment for the gym class scrawny klutz.

"What about transportation? You and dad are too busy with work."

"Aunt Agnes and your grandmother will be glad to pick you up and keep you with them until one of us is ready to get you."

Old ladies on top of sports camps. What a nightmare, he thought, contorting his face with displeasure as if he had swallowed a bottle of cough medicine.

"Consequences are not supposed to be pleasant, Zachariah. Second…"

"Hello," yelled his dad from the other end of the house. "Where's everybody?"

"In Zachariah's room," yelled back his mom.

"Second, there will be…"

"They didn't feed us this time," said his dad as he walked into the room, briefcase still in his hand. "I'm starving. What's for dinner?"

"We had PB&J sandwiches. You're welcome to go scavenge in the kitchen if PB&J doesn't appeal to you."

"What's wrong, sweetie?" he asked in a concerned tone.

"This boy is in big trouble."

"What happened?"

"I'll tell you later."

"You both look like the dog died. Tell me. Maybe I can help."

Cool, her agent is acting assertive for a change, thought Zach.

"I said I'll tell you later," she said impatiently. "It's complicated."

Realizing that including his dad would make things drag on forever without impacting the end result because Dad always agreed with Mom, Zach added, "Mom had a bad day today, and I didn't make it better."

"Okay, I'll go make a couple of sandwiches," he said, shrugging his shoulders. "Then I'll watch some TV."

"Back to your second consequence," Zach's mom said as soon as his dad left the room. "No Patrick for you from now until the end of summer vacation."

Zach didn't care much. First, he was too upset with Patrick to want to hang out with him anytime soon. Second, Patrick spent all the month of July with his grandparents in Chicago, three weeks in August at camp in Wisconsin, and one week on vacation with his parents somewhere out of town. That took care of most of the summer.

"Third, you'll clean the two bathrooms once a week for six weeks, starting this Saturday. Last, no computer for you until the end of the summer vacation, starting tonight. Don't you dare sneak, because that'll have its consequences."

The last punishment was the harshest and most horrifying. Zach desperately needed to stay in touch with Gem. He couldn't suddenly disappear and abandon her. She didn't need another blow and another disappointment. Samson was a good friend, and she shouldn't have to lose him.

"No, please, not the computer. I'll do anything just for thirty minutes of computer time twice a week. I'll clean the bathrooms, vacuum, sweep, mop, clean the windows, and take out the trash for the whole summer. Please, please, I'll do anything you want for just a little computer time."

His mother looked at him long and hard, her poker face morphing into a mixture of confusion, astonishment, weariness, and irritation.

"You sound desperate. You're willing to do all that for the whole summer for one hour of computer time a week. Consequences are not supposed to be fun, but you certainly went berserk over this one. What's all this about?"

Zach fidgeted with the button of his polo shirt without uttering a single word.

"Look, Zachariah, I'm worn-out. Either you tell me or I'm

taking the computer and going to bed."

"Well, at my school," he said hesitantly, "there's this tough girl. She beat me up. She slammed me against the lockers and shoved me onto the floor, bruising my hands."

"Why didn't you tell me?" she exclaimed with great frustration. "This kind of person should be in a special school for troubled, violent children."

"No, no. Gem is very nice."

"Now you're confusing me. One minute you say Gem beat you up, then the next, you say she's nice?"

"There's this other boy."

"You're not making any sense. Are you playing a game with my head?"

"No, no. He's kind of, sort of, almost like me."

"Did she beat him up too?"

"No, he helps soothe her. Now she gets into less trouble than before."

"You're still making no sense whatsoever."

"Samson and me are like, like…"

Waiting patiently, his mom looked at him quizzically as he fumbled with his words.

"Like me and Chad."

"What?" she said, jumping out of her seat.

Mrs. Higgins glared at her son.

"Alright, Melissa, take a deep breath," she said to herself. "It's one of those long, messy days."

Breathing deeply and exhaling slowly, she sat down again.

"Zachariah, how many fake lives do you have on Facebook?"

"Only two."

"Are you sure?"

"Really, truly, only two. I promise."

"And how are you going to die this time? From typhoid fever or is it the plague?"

"Samson isn't going to die."

"Ah, Samson, not you. Forgive my blunder. So, what's the master revenge plan?"

"See, it all started to get back at Gem after she beat me up. I wanted to become her friend and know more about her so I could find something to use against her. As I read her messages, I felt more and more sorry for her. Her life is so difficult, and she keeps getting one blow after another."

Seeing the interest on his mom's face, he added, "The best way to understand the whole thing is to go back and read all the messages."

"Good idea."

"The private messages are the most important ones," he said as he went to Samson's page.

She read all the private messages, her face looking sadder and more concerned with every message recounting Gem's misfortunes, her tongue clucking with every message recounting a misdeed."

"What a heartbreaking situation. Gem is acting up out of frustration. The crazy thing is that she got all these detentions, vandalized a locker, and you call that getting into less trouble. What did she do when she was always in trouble? Ah, well, perhaps Samson is moving her in the right direction. Unfortunately for you, Zachariah Kermit, a consequence is a consequence. However, I'll make a little exception. I'll let you have twenty minutes of computer time twice a week in four weeks."

"What? I won't be able to communicate with her for a month! It's not fair!"

"What you did to Billie wasn't fair, and I'm being lenient only for the sake of poor Gem," she said, before thoughtfully adding, "If her dad's hand would somehow get better, then everything would be fine."

"I'll seem flaky if I disappear all of a sudden then reappear weeks later. Gem will never have any more faith in me. I mean, Samson."

"Don't worry," she said as she started to type a private message to Gem, Zach helplessly watching.

Samson 112

Mom grounded me. No computers for 4 weeks. Talk to you in 4 weeks.

Just now

She clicked on send.

"All taken care of," she said, smiling. "As soon as you're able to use the computer again, you'll need to reveal your true identity.

You can't keep on deceiving her forever."

Zach nodded, too tired and too deflated to argue.

"Now I can get ready for bed after this horrendous day," she said, yawning.

Before leaving, she made sure to take the computer with her, carrying it like a trophy.

"Remember, you need to reveal your true identity," she called out from the hallway. "Doing it before you're able to use the computer would be even better."

Zach rolled his eyes.

"Nag, nag, nag, nag," he mumbled to himself.

A defeated Zach changed slowly into his pajamas and threw himself on the bed, leaving a pile of clothes on the floor, lying limp and neglected—the same way he felt on the inside. Despite his exhaustion, he was unable to sleep. In the darkness of his room, one thought repeated itself incessantly. *If only his right hand worked.*

Struck by a sudden revelation, Zach sat up in his bed.

CHAPTER 20

"Dr. Jackson," he screamed. "HE CAN FIX IT!"

Although his mother worked in a different part of the hospital, she had worked with Dr. Jackson for years during which the two families exchanged Christmas letters. He could ask his mother for help, but he felt determined to help Gem himself without relying on anybody else.

Zach listened for a while to ensure his screaming had not awakened his parents. The house was totally silent. Quietly and carefully, he went to his desk. He fumbled in the dark for his computer, but could not find it. Well, of course, his mom took it, so he turned on the desk lamp, tore a page from one of his notebooks, and started to write.

Dear Dr. Jackson,

My name is Zach. I'm thirteen years old. I've heard you are an excellent hand surgeon. I also heard that you travel every year for 2 weeks in the fall to Latin America and 2 weeks in the spring to Africa where you do free surgeries on the hands of poor people to help them go back to work.

A careless driver ran a red light and hit the car of the father of a girl at my school. As a result, his right hand is messed up and needs surgery. He badly needs two good hands because he's a mechanic, but he's too poor to afford the hand surgery. He has four kids, and the whole family is living in his mother's tiny apartment. Space is so tight the unlucky girl sleeps in the kitchen.

Can you please help? They really, really need you.

My address is on the back of the envelope.

Sincerely,

Zach Higgins

Quietly, Zach sneaked out of his room and into the office where he removed from the bottom shelf of the bookcase a green box labeled 2010 Holidays. He searched for Mrs. Jackson's letter, hoping his mother didn't throw away the envelope. Within a few minutes, Zach found a long red envelope from Mrs. Jackson. He wrote down the address on a piece of paper, then returned everything to the shelf. Before leaving the office, he grabbed an envelope and a stamp.

With a big smile of satisfaction on his face, Zach hid the ready-to-mail letter in the top drawer of his desk under a pile of papers. The clock on his night table read 2:11 a.m.

Friday, June 3

With the first ring of his alarm, Zach woke up ready for a new day. Despite a short sleep, hope energized him.

The first time he ran into Billie, she glared at him for a brief moment before hissing, "At least it was you and not a fifty-year-old pervert. I can't believe how I was hurrying to go to his house." After that, she treated him like a total stranger, looking straight through him whenever they coincidently ran into each other. During lunch, she focused on her friends, totally ignoring his table. She unquestionably was set on protecting her beauty. What he had blurted out during a moment of despair about grudges being beauty destroyers achieved great unintended results.

Except for Billie's puffy eyes, she looked decent given all she had gone through the last couple of days.

***

When he returned home in the afternoon, he rode his bike to the mailbox where he dropped off his letter to Dr. Jackson. He hoped with all his heart that Dr. Jackson would agree to help and not toss the letter in the trash.

Monday–Thursday, June 6–9

The last four days of school were a mixture of finals, a little teaching, movies, ice cream, and fun games. Billie appeared to be still protecting her beauty by totally ignoring Zach.

Friday, June 10

Summer vacation at last. The first day, Zach slept in and ate a candy bar for breakfast. What the heck, his mom was at work. He watched cartoons until noon when his grandmother, known as Nanny, took him to his favorite place, Pine City Bread Company. There, she had no problem indulging him with fried chicken and a big chocolate fudge cookie. Nanny wanted to take him to her house for a swim, but he was anxious to return home to check the mail. The mailman always came to their house between noon and 1:00.

Letters and catalogs filled the mailbox. Zach grabbed an envelope that caught his attention, a fancy beige one.

"Yes!" he shouted. "It's from Dr. Jackson."

A passerby turned his head to see what was going on. Too impatient to take the letter inside, he tore open the envelope, his heart pounding, and he read the letter typed on fancy beige paper.

June 8, 2011

Dear Zach,

I was delighted to receive your letter. You must be Melissa's son. Your letter reminded me of her. You both have the same conviction and drive to help those in need. You must have inherited a lot from her. It is unfortunate she moved to the heart hospital. Since she moved across the street, I haven't even run into her.

I'll be happy to help your classmate's father regain the functionality in his injured hand. I perform surgeries for free in foreign countries, and I have no hesitation helping a fellow American. In the U.S., the medical system is more complicated than in Africa and Latin America, but I promise to do my best and use my influence to get him substantial discounts from the entities outside my office, like the hospital, the lab, and so on. All he has to do is call my office (I have enclosed my business card). I will inform my staff about him, and I will try my best to squeeze him into my schedule and perform whatever is needed as soon as possible.

Give my regards to your mother. She is an outstanding

nurse.

Sincerely,
Edgar L. Jackson, M.D.

Zach's heart swelled with joy. Although that thing about being a lot like his mother didn't settle well with Zach, he decided not to dwell on it, because the doctor had never met him to know how different he and his mother were. Dr. Jackson not running into his mother since she moved to the heart hospital was reassuring; she was not likely to know anything from the doctor or his staff for a very, very long time—perhaps never.

Letter in hand, he ran into the house, leaving the rest of the mail in the box. Now, how was he going to deliver the incredible news to Gem and her father? Should he send a letter? From whom? Samson? No, it wouldn't work. Once her dad saw Dr. Jackson, the whole truth would emerge, and Gem would know Samson's real identity. Although he had promised his mom and had the intention to tell Gem the truth about Samson, he wanted to control the timing of his confession. From Zach? Wouldn't it seem odd for Zach to go through all that effort after all the bad things Gem did to him? Besides, how did he find out about her dad's hand when nobody at school knew much about Gem's personal life? Would her dad even take the letter seriously? No. He needed another way!

On the deck, Zach rocked in the rocking chair for a long time as he thought about his next step. The importance and urgency of revealing his true identity sneaked into his thoughts, both complicating and simplifying his decision. A phone call would be the best way to achieve both purposes. He would first tell her the good news then confess. Hopefully, her happiness and appreciation for what he did for her father would make her more forgiving. The phone call would also allow them to have a conversation. It worked well with Billie, and it would probably work with Gem. It was worth a try.

Inside the house, he searched in the school directory for Gem Bardel. He found nothing. Bummer! Where was he supposed to find her phone number? Frustrated and confused, he threw himself on the couch and sat gazing at the dark TV screen for a long time until he remembered Grandma Cordelia. Yes, Gem's grandmother must be

Cordelia Bardel. Nanny dialed the operator whenever she wanted to find out a phone number. She did that during their lunch today. He had to find out the operator's number.

He ran across the street and rang the Marvins' door bell. Mr. Marvin opened the door.

"Hello, Mr. Marvin," said Zach with a smile.

"Hello," said Mr. Marvin, reciprocating the smile. "What are you selling today? Cookie dough or chocolate?"

"Neither. I just want to know the number of the operator who helps people find phone numbers."

"Aren't you going to app it?" he asked, trying to sound like an expert on computer lingo although his tone was laced with sarcasm.

"My computer isn't working right," Zach said, trying hard to suppress a giggle and keep a straight face.

"There is nothing better than the old proven ways."

"Exactly."

"You know, the operator can help you find any phone number. All you have to do is dial the area code then 555-1212 and give the name of the person or business you want to call. Easy."

"Very," said Zach. "Thank you very much."

"Anything else I can help you with?"

"No, thanks."

"Give my regards to your parents."

"I will," said Zach as he ran back home.

CHAPTER 21

Gathering every ounce of courage, Zach dialed Cordelia Bardel's phone number.

"Hello," said a screechy voice.

"I'm Zach. Me and Gem go to the same school. "

"You need to raise your voice. I'm a little hard of hearing."

Zach repeated what he had just said, raising his voice.

"School?" she said, surprise apparent in her voice. "No, this is a home, not a school."

Frustrated, Zach yelled the same thing at the top of his lungs, adding, "Can I speak to Gem?"

"Gem is babysitting. She'll be back a little after five. She babysits on Mondays, Wednesdays, and Fridays, from eight to five. All the other times, she's usually here."

"Thank you," he yelled as loud as he could.

"I'll let her know you called, Ezekiel."

"Ezekiel?" said Zach to himself as soon as he hung up. "I'll stick with Zachariah, thank you. Yikes. This woman is deaf."

Zach thought it was a bummer Gem wasn't home when he was all psyched up to talk to her, but after a while, he started to think maybe it wasn't too bad he couldn't speak to her. Perhaps the good news about her dad's hand was not good enough to guarantee her forgiveness when he revealed that Samson was a fabrication. She may be too upset to move on as if nothing had happened. Perhaps he needed to speak to her father when she's at work, then after the good news had sunk in for a couple of days, he'd call her and confess.

He grabbed the phone and started to dial Cordelia's number, but stopped midway. Perhaps it would be better to deliver the news to Gem's father face-to-face. That was the best way, he decided, but he didn't know her grandmother's address. He thought for a while before remembering that Cordelia lived in an apartment building with "deluxe" and another word in its name. No matter how hard he tried, he couldn't remember what the other word was.

He grabbed the telephone book and looked in the yellow pages under "Apartments." He turned page after page, reading the names of apartment buildings and highlighting all the ones with "deluxe" and another word in their names. How slow and cumbersome life was before Google. Fortunately, only two buildings fit these criteria: Tuscan Deluxe Apartments and Serenity Deluxe Apartments. At the end of the section on apartments, both had detailed advertisements. Serenity Apartments advertised themselves as having spacious apartments in a quiet wooded area with a gym and swimming pool on site. The advertisement for Tuscan Apartments provided a list of appealing features: cozy apartments, all utilities included, balconies, close to shopping, restaurants, grocery store, and bus stop in front of the building. Many of the descriptions for the Tuscan Apartments seemed to match what Gem had mentioned in one of her messages.

Saturday, June 11

Zach rode his bike to the convenience store where he examined the pamphlets for the city bus schedule. He stuffed in his pocket a pamphlet for bus 53.

Monday, June 13

Bus 53 stopped a few blocks away from his house every two hours. Without his parents' knowledge, Zach walked to the bus stop to catch the 10:00 a.m. bus. Riding the bus for the first time felt like a great adventure. With a mixture of excitement and apprehension, Zach waited at the stop, but no bus arrived at 10:00. The woman sitting on the bench, probably waiting for the same bus, didn't seem concerned as she quietly read her book. Twelve minutes later, the bus finally arrived. Zach leaped onto the bus, eager to get going. The other passenger stood up slowly and ambled towards the bus. Even after the slow woman seated herself, the late bus remained stopped for a few minutes as if waiting for more riders. *What's wrong with this stupid driver?* thought Zach as he nervously bit his nails. *What is he waiting for? All the passengers should have been at the stop over fifteen minutes ago.*

Whenever the bus approached a stop, the driver called out its name. The bus made many stops, too many. Zach felt anxious, as he wanted to reach his destination before losing his nerve. Unfortunately, he didn't own the bus, and the driver wasn't his private chauffeur. All the stops were way too long, Zach felt, but some stretched more than others, depending on the number of passengers leaving and boarding, loading and unloading bikes off the rack mounted to the front of the bus.

Finally, the driver called out Tuscan, omitting "deluxe" and "apartments." His manners forgotten, Zach ran to the door and jumped out of the bus, totally ignoring the other passengers trying to leave or board. He stormed into the building. Once inside, he realized the obvious—apartment buildings, unlike houses, housed many families. He had no idea in which apartment Gem lived. He wondered if he should knock on every door until he found the right apartment, but wasn't that kind of dangerous? As he stood in the entrance pondering his problem, he noticed a set of mailboxes mounted on the wall, each with an apartment number and a slot for the resident's name. Many slots were empty, but apartment eleven's box had the name Cordelia Bardel neatly handwritten on a yellowing piece of paper. Bingo! He had hit the jackpot!

Zach stood in front of apartment eleven for a while before lifting his right arm to knock on the door. When his fist almost touched the door, he put down his right arm and raised his left. Zach switched arms several times as he grew more and more nervous, and the task grew more and more monumental with every attempt. Perhaps some fresh air would help him regain his composure, he reasoned. He couldn't just give up after coming all this way.

Outside the building, Zach took a few deep breaths as he examined the houses across the street. They were old, but mostly well-maintained and were different shapes, sizes, and colors, unlike the cookie-cutter houses in his neighborhood. When he turned around, he saw a two-story box-shaped structure with a drab white exterior and a red-slanted roof, far from deluxe. It stood between a U-shaped brick building to its left and a strip-mall to its right.

Zach strolled around the mall, reading the sign on every store and lingering in front of their windows. He convinced himself that procrastination would rebuild his lost courage, enabling him to meet with a man he hardly knew.

The store closest to the apartments was Super Mart, another branch of the grocery store where his mother shopped. It was Double Coupon Day.

The Nag-a-Lot, he thought, *will definitely stop by their store after work to take advantage of the great offer. We'll be eating some of the same trash over and over. Yuck.*

Yummy Hamburgers was next. He had never heard of this place before Gem told him about it. Linda's Alterations seemed more attractive with its headless, legless mannequin displaying a black dress with a large beaded American flag on its front. He moved on to Clarity Phones with its display of different styles of cell phones. A big banner behind the glass read: $39.99 Unlimited Talk and Text. The smell of Oriental food filled Zach's nostrils—it was New China Super Buffet. On the door, a big, yellow smiley face stared at him. Zach recoiled in disgust.

"Oh, no. Not that thing again," Zach mumbled to himself. "Billie has smiley-faced me out."

Quickly he moved to the next shop: Fabulous Hair Salon. A thick red curtain covered the store's window, making the inside totally invisible. A list of services was displayed on the glass: cut, color, foiling, waxing, and facials. How boring! To Zach, a haircut always meant tons of nagging before he succumbed to the ordeal. He often wished he wore a hearing aid so he could turn it off when his mother started her nagging. Ned's Shoe Repair was next. An old man, probably Ned, hunched over a low bench, hammering his tacks into the heel of a boot. He watched for a while before moving to the last store, Three Brothers Pawn Shop. Like all pawn shops, black, heavy iron bars protected the vulnerable glass front. A large poster of the three smiling, big-bellied, middle-aged men was taped to the window with WE TAKE GOOD CARE OF OUR CUSTOMERS' NEEDS printed in large bold letters above it. The men in the photograph looked like prison inmates. One of them seemed to have a scar on his face. Their faces suggested a cryptic, creepy meaning to the sentence printed above their picture. Zach suspected these guys doubled as hit men.

A few yards away, stood Barbecue Shack, a detached, small stand at the end of the parking lot close to the road. The inviting, smoky aroma of the meat convinced Zach that a bit of food would boost his courage.

Barbecue sandwich in hand, he walked back to the apartment building, unaware of the barbecue sauce dripping all over his white T-shirt with every bite. This time, he was ready. He walked with purpose down the hall. Quickly, he knocked twice on the door, hoping his courage would not betray him.

CHAPTER 22

A tall, burly, and scruffy man opened the door.

"Yes?" he inquired dryly, his face stern and uninviting.

Intimidated, Zach stood frozen, his mouth dry and his tongue paralyzed.

"What do you want?" he impatiently asked as he ran his fingers through his thick black hair.

"I, I g-g-go to school with G-gem," Zach barely managed to utter.

"She's not here," he said, his tone so hostile that Zach grew even more nervous and less able to talk without stuttering.

"I, I c-c-came to see you."

Mr. Bardel made a slow complete turn. Zach noticed his immobilized claw-like right hand with fingers slightly separated and considerably turned inward.

"Now, you have seen the whole of me."

"I m-m-meant to say t-t-talk to you."

Smirking sarcastically, Mr. Bardel examined the terrified Zach.

"Go ahead," he finally said. "I'm all ears."

"Do you know Dr. Edgar Jackson?"

"I've heard of him."

"He's a f-famous h-h-hand surgeon."

"Aha."

"He's g-going to f-f-fix your h-h-hand for f-free."

"And I'm going to teach him to walk on water for free," Mr. Bardel said, grinning widely, his eyes playfully wicked, but his voice abrasively cold.

Despite Zach's disappointment and unease, he pushed on, "I'm, I'm s-serious."

"Son, go play somewhere else."

"I have the p-proof," said Zach, frantically looking through the many pockets of his cargo shorts for Dr. Jackson's letter.

Mr. Bardel watched him, his face stony, his eyes narrowed. Zach didn't find any letter, so he went through his pockets again, slowly and more carefully. Still nothing. He almost died from embarrassment. How could he have come all this way without the proof?

"I, I must have l-l-left it at h-h-home," he hiccuped his words, feeling like a total idiot.

"Sure, you have the big fat PROOOOF. Go play your pranks somewhere else," Mr. Bardel said firmly and angrily, his bear-like figure looming over Zach. "I have enough to deal with. Don't need little children playing dirty jokes on me."

Terrified, Zach backed up, mumbling his apologies before turning around and walking away, his heart heavy with sadness. His mission had gone bust. What a lousy helper he was.

***

Zach shuffled into the house after another long ride on a crowded bus. The mere presence of all those people suffocated him. Endless stops interrupted the ride. During each stop, Zach wished he could grow wings, burst through the window, and fly home.

Dr. Jackson's letter sat unfolded next to its envelope on his bed. The sight of the letter pained him so much; he wished he were dead. The second shock awaited him when he caught a glimpse of himself in the bathroom mirror. The dried barbecue sauce encrusted on his chin and sides of his mouth and the big reddish stains scattered all over the front of his white T-shirt devastated him.

"How presentable I look," he hissed. "Like a messy toddler."

Depressed and defeated, Zach curled up on the couch, gazing into the empty fireplace, his mind blank, his body numb. Hours later, his dad arrived carrying two bags of Chinese take-out.

"Are you okay?" he asked when he noticed Zach lying listlessly on the couch.

"Yeah," replied Zach in a faint voice.

"Sure?" asked his dad as he placed the bags of food on the kitchen table.

"Yeah."

His dad shrugged his shoulders.

"I need to get out of this hot suit," he said, as he walked down the hall. "If you need anything, just holler."

Minutes later, his mom walked in hauling multiple grocery bags. Manically happy, as she always was when she came back from Super Mart on a Double Coupon Day, she placed her bags on the kitchen table before returning to the garage for a second and final time. So caught up in her frenzied excitement, she did not notice Zach lying still on the couch like a potato sack.

"What's all that?" her husband asked when she walked into the house with her second load of bags.

"You won't believe all the great deals at Super Mart today," she said with the excitement of a child after a successful evening of trick-or-treating.

"I can see," he said pointing to the bags.

"That's not all. I put the three turkeys in the garage freezer."

"Three turkeys? We'll be all turkeyed-out by Thanksgiving. Your mother won't like our lukewarm attitude towards her turkey."

"We're having Thanksgiving at your mom's and Christmas in New York this year."

"Of course, our reaction won't matter when it is my mom's turkey," he said playfully.

"She prepares such a large spread. The turkey is just another dish. Anyway, stop griping and help me put all these things away, so we'll have space to eat on."

"Pantyhose?" Zach's dad said when he picked up the first bag, surprise apparent in his voice. "Since when do you wear pantyhose, Melissa?"

"Since next winter, Gregory. Ten pairs of Antonio Barberini hose for $14.99. No way was I going to pass that up. It's not a deal; it's a steal."

"I can't believe you. You're a shopaholic!"

She took her loot to the bedroom, returning rapidly to help her husband unpack. Quickly and efficiently, they put away the ridiculous amounts of stuff: thirty-six rolls of toilet paper, twelve cans of light cream of mushroom soup, ten bags of frozen green beans, eight jars of meat-flavored spaghetti sauce, and thirty cans of tuna. As Zach had predicted earlier in the day, they were going to eat the same foods over and over for weeks to come.

After they put away the groceries and the frenzied excitement of Double Coupon Day gradually fizzled out; Mr. Higgins told his wife that Zach was curled up on the sofa and didn't look quite right.

"He probably has the pre-basketball camp blues," she said casually. "You know how much he hates sports."

"Yup."

"He's paying for his actions," she said in a grave voice. "Anyway, a few stronger muscles won't hurt him."

"You think he's coming down with yellow fever?"

"Probably Malta fever. It tends to stick around for a while, most likely until his summer camps are over."

"How convenient!"

They both laughed heartily. Zach heard every word, but absolutely nothing mattered to him. Under different circumstances, he would have protested and accused them of cruelty.

"Dinner time," Mr. Higgins called. "Zachariah, I got your favorite, sweet and sour chicken."

"Not hungry."

"Come on, Zachariah, let's have a nice family dinner," his dad said. "Basketball camp isn't that horrible."

Zach didn't answer.

Determined to lure him to the dinner table, his mom walked into the living room chanting, "Sweet and sour chicken, sweet and sour chicken. Yummy, yummy. Sweet and sour chicken, sweet and sour chicken, sweet and sour chicken. Yummy, yummy."

As soon as she saw her son's face, she realized it was more serious than the basketball blues.

"Oh, little Zachy," she said, using a nickname she used only when Zach was in great distress. "You look miserable. What's wrong?"

Not bothering to complain about her use of a babyish name, something he had consistently been doing since he was seven, he mumbled, "Nothing."

Kneeling next to the couch, she placed her lips on his forehead to check his temperature. No fever.

"There must be something," she whispered, playfully ruffling his hair, as his dad stood watching near the doorway.

He gave her a blank look.

"Look at you. You look terrible," she said, her voice getting louder and more frantic with every word. For a few minutes, she stood still, watching her son, waiting for a reaction, but getting only blank looks.

"Come on, don't you want to tell Mommy who loves you and cares about you?"

Still no answer. For a while, she knelt next to him, caressing his hair and chanting softly, "Mommy and Daddy love little Zacky."

Providing an escape to much simpler times, all that babying soothed Zach rather than upset him as it had always done for the past few years. He closed his eyes. Unintentionally, tears rolled down his cheeks.

"How about some juicy?"

Without waiting for an answer, she kissed his wet cheek and then headed to the kitchen where she retrieved a cup of juice. She hurried to the living room followed by her husband, who took his former position near the doorway. Zach's mom kneeled next to him again. Unexpectedly, he clung to her neck like a baby chimp, weeping, shaking, spilling part of the juice on her scrubs. His dad rushed and took the cup from her hand, allowing her to hug her son and rub his back, while he caressed Zach's hair with his free hand. Zach's sobs slowly diminished until they subsided. He let go of his mother's neck and squirmed, signaling the end of the embrace. His mother moved away and stood up.

"Come on, sweetie," she said as Zach's father returned to his former spot near the doorway, cup still in hand. "Let's eat and discuss what's bothering you."

"I don't want to eat or talk," he said, exhaustion apparent in his voice. "I just want to sleep."

"At least have a few bites and open up a tiny bit. It's not good for you to go to bed on an empty stomach with a bunch of bottled up worries."

"Let the boy sleep," said his father. "A skipped meal won't kill him, and he'll open up when he's ready."

Mrs. Higgins threw her arms up in the air. "Okay," she said tentatively.

The affection Zach received from his parents filled him with confidence, creating within him a desire to confront that intimidating Bardel. He messed up the first time, but he was going to do it right the second time.

CHAPTER 23

Wednesday, June 15

Wearing his Sunday best, Zach secretly rode the bus to Cordelia Bardel's apartment when Gem was at work. He heard the loud TV as he knocked on the apartment's door with great determination. Mr. Bardel, dressed in gray shorts and a tattered, oversized T-shirt with a design so faded it was unrecognizable, opened the door.

"Look who's back," he said dryly, inquisitively examining Zach and his elegant suit. "The stutterer."

"My name is Zachariah Higgins," he said assertively, using his long, old-fashioned name to add heft to his small size.

"Oh, excuse me for forgetting your famous name," Mr. Bardel said, smirking. "By the way, I love your clip-on tie."

Zach felt his calm slipping away, but he was determined not to allow the man to derail him with his rudeness.

"I'm here to discuss Dr. Jackson's offer, not what I'm wearing," said Zach as emphatically as he could

"The free surgery?" said Mr. Bardel, rolling his eyes

"Yes, sir."

"Again?" said Mr. Bardel, sighing in an exaggerated manner. "Zachariah, I already told you to go play your games somewhere else."

"Sir, this is not a game. Just give me a few minutes of your time, and I'll explain and prove everything."

Again Mr. Bardel sighed loudly but didn't utter a single word.

"Sir, can I come in?" asked Zach, taking advantage of the brief silence.

"Sir, you may come in," said Mr. Bardel with a smirk, his eyes wickedly playful.

They went through a short, dim hallway, leading into a small, messy living room with an odd smell reminiscent of spoiled milk. A white-haired old woman wearing glasses and connected to a portable oxygen tank was dozing off on the couch facing an old TV.

"Can we turn off the TV or at least turn down the volume?"

"No, we cannot. My mom loves Westerns."

"She's asleep."

"She looks like that when she's sucked into a show she loves."

"Can we go somewhere else then?"

"Nope, we cannot. I'm only comfortable on my daddy's old recliner, may his soul rest in peace," he said, pointing to a bulky recliner with a sunken seat, covered with a shabby, checkered fabric. "You know, it's also a pullout bed and so is the couch. Practical furniture is the best."

Frustrated by Mr. Bardel's behavior, Zach sat on the other end of the couch, where the lady was dozing, determined not to let this wacky man have the pleasure of intimidating him with his negative attitude.

"Zachariah, please start talking," he said, with the same smirk on his lips and wicked playfulness in his eyes that had never left his face since Zach had entered the apartment. Before Zach said anything, he added, "If you may allow me to say, all this politeness is making us sound like we're some stuffy, old English aristocrats. I'm the Earl of Reality, and you're the Duke of Tall-Tales."

Zach's face felt hot. He tried to maintain his composure and hoped his face didn't give him away.

"Well, to…"

"We have a visitor," Cordelia unexpectedly chimed in gleefully.

"This is Zachariah Higgins. He's claiming a famous doctor wants to do surgery on my hand for free. Imagine, a doctor who wants no money," said Mr. Bardel in a booming voice to his hard-of-hearing mother.

"It's true. It's true," shouted Zach as he pulled the envelope from his jacket's inner pocket and handed it to Cordelia.

Cordelia eagerly took the envelope, examined it, then pulled out the letter and read it.

"It's fake," yelled Mr. Bardel.

Zach dug his fingers into the protruding foam of a cushion

next to him, trying to dissipate his anger.

"Oh, honey, don't listen to him," she said looking at Zach with pleading eyes. "He needs all the help he can get. His right hand is crippled. I'm sure whoever smashed Rob's car was all liquored-up."

A mixture of sadness and anger filled her son's face as if her words had brought back all the bad memories.

"I'll make some lemonade," she said as she stood up and smoothed her faded, flowery housecoat.

"You don't have to miss part of the movie," yelled Mr. Bardel. "He'll be leaving soon."

Leaving the open letter on the sofa, Cordelia shuffled out of the room, rolling her oxygen tank in front of her. Zach wasn't sure whether the mother didn't hear her son or chose to ignore him, but he felt encouraged.

"To make a long story short, boy, what prank are you playing or what are you on?" he asked, his question dripping with anger and mistrust.

Mr. Bardel's behavior, starting with the evasive teasing and wicked playfulness and ending with outright anger and rude insults, infuriated Zach.

"This isn't a prank. Somebody really wants to help you get better. And if I'm on anything, it's the faith in the goodness inside people's hearts," Zach answered, the intensity of his emotions apparent in his voice.

"Go ahead, Zachariah, say what you came here to say, but you better not try to bamboozle me," he said, sounding more serious and ready to cooperate.

Mr. Bardel's sudden change in attitude surprised Zach. Perhaps it was the sincerity Mr. Bardel detected in his voice. Instead of dwelling on the reasons, Zach seized the opportunity to accomplish his goal. He smiled and raised his right hand.

"I promise to tell the truth only."

Mr. Bardel grinned, seeming amused and more relaxed.

"Me and Gem go to the same school and are in the same French class. I found out you had a car accident and were badly hurt. You recovered, but your right hand needed a surgery you couldn't afford. Your hurt hand kept you from working. You lost your house, your dog, your lifestyle. Now the six of you are living with your mom in this tiny apartment. I wanted so much to help. I had heard my mom, who's a nurse, talk about Dr. Jackson's travels to Africa and South America to do free surgeries on the hands of people like you who can't work because their hands are messed up. I wrote Dr. Jackson a letter to ask for help. This is the reply. Go ahead—read it, and figure out for yourself if I'm trying to bamboozle you or not," Zach said quickly, barely taking a breath, fearing an interruption at any moment.

As Mr. Bardel read the letter, his mother walked in rolling her oxygen tank in one hand and carrying a pitcher of lemonade in the other. Smiling shyly, Gina followed her, carrying a stack of empty glasses. Gem's young sister piled some of the junk on one side of the coffee table on top of the clothes and food wrappers cluttering the other end of the table, creating a space for the pitcher and glasses. She ran out of the room immediately after placing down the glasses, softly mumbling her greetings.

"Excuse our mess," said Cordelia in a weak, raspy voice as she put down the pitcher. "Them boys are messy."

Cordelia collapsed on the couch, wheezing. Zach gave her a worried look.

"I'll be okay in a minute," she said breathlessly.

Immediately, Zach filled the glasses with lemonade, giving the first one to the old lady.

"Thank you, honey," she said, sounding a little breathless. "I'm so embarrassed. I should be serving you."

"Don't worry about it," yelled Zach.

"You're so kind," the old woman said with a smile, her wrinkled face beaming with gratitude. "Carrying the pitcher was a bit too much for me."

Zach took a sip of his lemonade.

"Delicious. Thank you."

"It's a secret recipe from the diner where I worked for forty-three years."

"I'll be able to work again," gushed Mr. Bardel, his voice quivering, his eyes dreamy.

"It's a great deal, isn't it?" Zach said.

"Yes, absolutely. I'm so sorry I gave you a rough time."

"I can understand. You've been hearing only bad news since the accident. When the offer of a free surgery suddenly popped up, it seemed like a trick. Now you believe me. That's what matters. The first thing you need to do is set an appointment with Dr. Jackson. This is his business card."

Mr. Bardel took the card and left the room. He returned after a few minutes with a smile on his face.

"I'm so lucky," he said, his voice shaking, his eyes glittering with tears. "My appointment is next Monday at 10:15."

"That's fast."

"They had a cancellation."

Gem's dad sat on his recliner and covered his face with his hands as if to absorb the overload of information thrown at him all at once.

Zach looked at Cordelia. She was asleep. For a while, both sipped their lemonades in silence.

"There's one thing I'd like to know, Zachariah," Mr. Bardel said, looking at Zach with curiosity. "How did you know about our situation? Gem is not a talker. I don't think she ever told anybody about our hardships, not even her closest friends. How did a person I've never heard of know all those details?"

Although Zach was planning to confess to Gem at a later time about his deceitful game, her father's curiosity took him by surprise. Intimidated, Zach swallowed hard, but he decided to be frank. While Cordelia drifted in and out of slumber, Zach told Gem's dad the whole story, watching his every facial expression, hoping the prospect of getting his life back would soften the impact of some parts of the long, convoluted story. Mr. Bardel listened intently, his face sometimes looking neutral; other times slightly amused.

"You children can be so ridiculous sometimes," he said with a smile when Zach was finally done.

Zach nodded in agreement, feeling a heavy weight lift off his shoulders.

While Gem's father's relaxed reaction relieved Zach, he felt bad when the joy on Mr. Bardel's face changed into apprehension.

"You and your family have gone through very hard times, but now it's almost over. Just hang in there for a couple of months, and everything will be good again," Zach said, in an attempt to cheer up Mr. Bardel. To Zach's shock, it dawned on him that he sounded like his mother. That was kind of freaky.

"You're right," he said, a smile lighting up his face. "Zachariah, I'll tell Gem all about your visit when she gets home from babysitting."

Zach was relieved. Somebody close to Gem, who felt sympathetic towards him, would be telling her the whole story. In a day or two, he'd call her to apologize. Hopefully, after she had some time to digest and internalize the whole thing, her reaction would be as favorable as her father's.

CHAPTER 24

Thursday, June 16

Throughout the day, Zach came up with one excuse after another to delay calling Gem. In the morning, it was too early. After all, kids slept in during the summer. In the afternoon, he needed to eat a snack, take the trash out, do this, that, and the other, finish watching this TV show, and then another and another. In the evening, he was too tired or too busy.

Thursday, June 30

Fifteen days had passed, and Zach had come up with various excuses to postpone contacting Gem. Being out of the house, being too tired, or being too stressed were among his many excuses. June 30th, however, was different. His grounding from the computer was over, at least partially, allowing him to communicate with Gem without having to talk to her directly. His mother had set the rules the night before. After returning from work and only using her laptop, she allowed Zach twenty minutes of computer time twice a week on Mondays and Thursdays. Zach begged to double his computer time, but his mother refused, making it clear he shouldn't waste his breath on something that would never happen. Seeing her determination, he gave up haggling.

When Zach's mom gave him her laptop, he immediately went to Samson's Facebook where he found two private messages from Gem.

Before I send her any apologies, I might as well check her messages, he thought.

Gem Bardel

Hi, whoever U are.

Whoever U are, my dad told me about your visit and all that happened. THANX 4 helping him fix his hand.

Now we R even. Your bad and my bad erased each other. All is cool between us.

Yesterday Dad saw Dr. Jackson. Cuz his injury is kind of old, he has a 50/50 chance of improving 100%. Bummer! But, he'll get at least some benefit. Dad told us he's looking forward 2 the surgery, but I can tell he's nervous and worried about not being able 2 work on cars again.

Thanx 4 not ratting on me when I invaded Victoria's locker. U have a good heart. I could have been kicked out from school. Someone like Victoria isn't worth taking such a risk over. I don't know what we were thinking.

U know what? I kind of like this Samson game. Let's keep on playing it. Whenever your punishment is over, please send more public wrestling links. U R like a genius at finding funny ones.

June 21 at 5:10 p.m.

Gem Bardel

Today is surgery day. The whole family, including Grandma Cordelia and her oxygen tank, arrived at the hospital at 6:00 in the morning. His surgery was supposed 2 last 1 hour but ended up lasting an extra 20 minutes. Dr. Jackson explained why the delay happened, but nobody understood much of what he said. He talks funny. I think he was trying 2 tell us he found some tangled up stuff that he had 2 untangle. Anyway, it all went well. He's now in the recovery room. In 1 or 2 hours we'll take him home, and he'll start some kind of hand rehab therapy in 1 or 2 weeks. This rehab should help him get much better a lot faster. The main thing is 2 stick with it and not get frustrated and quit. Quitting worries me the most cuz since the accident, Dad started 2 get frustrated and quit very easily.

This place is like WOW. They have computers in the waiting room 4 us 2 use. That's where I'm writing my message. They also have snacks and drinks. This hospital is the bomb.

When will your grounding end? Your mom's punishments are nasty!

9 hours ago

After reading Gem's messages, Zach's feelings were all mixed up. Although relieved, her casual reaction to his deception surprised him. He was expecting a stronger reaction even if she didn't get outright angry. Her idea of two bad things erasing each other, and her desire to continue playing the Samson game astonished him. She was odd, but kind of cute. Her family seemed like a bunch of oddballs. Besides, the uncertainties surrounding the healing of Mr. Bardel's hand agitated him.

For the rest of his computer time, he posted a funny wrestling video on her wall and then sent her a private message.

Samson 112
Hi,
My computer grounding is kind of over. Can use it 4 twenty minutes on Mondays and Thursdays. Bummer!
U r right. When my mom gets mad, she can come up with some nasty punishments. She takes away what I like and dumps on me what I don't. U also haven't heard her nag. It is her favorite activity. I bet if they had a world championship in nagging, she'd win the gold medal.
Glad everything is cool between us after our 2 bads erased each other. Still want 2 apologize 4 lying to you even though something good came out of the whole mess.
Happy ur dad's surgery is over. Hope he'll be one of those lucky 50% who recover 100%.
Hope u'll like my link.

Just now

A haze surrounded Zack's brain all evening. When he went to bed, sleep seemed as unattainable as his mother giving up nagging. When sleep finally came, it was fragmented and restless.

Wednesday, July 6

Since he had read the last two messages from Gem, Zach had been feeling an urgency to come clean with his parents, too. It wasn't because he was scared his mom would find out everything he had hidden and would punish him more. It was something deeper—a vague, gnawing, lingering sensation growing more relentless every day. Too chicken to confess directly to his parents, he wrote a letter, made two copies, kept the original for himself and placed each copy in an envelope. He left the envelope addressed to his dad on the desk in the office and the one addressed to his mom on top of her dresser.

Zach started his letter by writing, "Mom and Dad, remember that evening when I cried a lot and then went to bed early without eating dinner? I did not tell you why I was upset on that day. Today, I want to tell you how sorry I am for leaving you all confused and worried. I'm also ready to tell you everything.

Mom, remember that time when you read all of Gem's messages to Samson? On that day, you said that if Gem's dad's hand would get better, then their problems would be solved. When I went to bed, I could not stop thinking about what you said. Suddenly, I remembered that Dr. Jackson is a great hand surgeon who does free surgeries in poor countries. I sent him a letter asking for his help. He agreed to help Gem's dad in his reply letter."

Zach then proceeded to write in great detail about his first visit to Gem's father, how deflating defeat felt, how their love on that evening of tears and desperation had given him the strength and the desire to accomplish his mission no matter what. He described how he revisited Mr. Bardel and succeeded in convincing him to see Dr. Jackson. He finished his letter with the news about Mr. Bardel's surgery and the importance of his upcoming hand rehabilitation program in improving his chances of a 100% recovery.

That evening, they ate an uninteresting tuna casserole dinner for the third time since Double Coupon Day. What a bore! About an hour later, Zach's dad rushed out of his office in a state of frenzied excitement, waving a couple of papers.

"Melissa," he screamed, "come, see your son's brilliance. I'm so proud of him."

Zach figured out immediately that his father was referring to his letter. Initially, Mr. Higgins's excitement had surprised Zach because he thought only his mom was capable of such hysterics. However, it did not take him long to smile with satisfaction.

"Come on," his dad continued to shout. "Where are you?"

"Just let me shove this bottle under the sink," Zach's mom yelled back.

Zach stayed in the living room watching TV while keeping an ear on the developments in the adjacent room.

Nothing seemed to be happening as silence prevailed in the nearby room. Unable to bear anymore suspense, Zach joined his parents in the dining room. Both were sitting at the table, his mother staring at the letter, a hint of a mysterious something on her face.

When his father noticed him, he left his seat, walked in Zach's direction and patted him twice on the back. He then wrapped one arm around his son's shoulders and gave him a squeeze.

"We all knew that fixing the man's hand would turn their lives around," his father said, "but you were the only one who remembered Dr. Jackson's charity work. Not even your mom remembered him despite having worked with him for years. You then took it several steps further. You asked the doctor for help then pushed and pushed until you convinced Gem's dad to cooperate. I'm more than impressed!"

Zach grinned broadly with pride and satisfaction, returning his dad's shoulder squeeze. However, when he saw his mom still scrutinizing the papers in front of her, he worried.

She surely must have read it at least once, he thought. *Why all this gazing? What is she up to?*

Finally, she turned around and looked at Zach. Zach's heart sank when he saw anger in her eyes.

"Zachariah, how dare you sneak behind our ba..."

"The boy is being honest," interrupted his dad. "Look at all the positives before pouncing on him."

Wow, thought Zach. *Dad is not parroting her. He now has his personal opinion.*

"I've read his letter three times," she said, turning her head in her husband's direction, glaring angrily at him. "I'm aware of all the positives and glad the poor man has a shot at recovery." Then she added, shifting her angry glare in her son's direction, "But, Zachariah, why all the secrecy?"

"I wanted to be Gem's only helper," replied Zach calmly.

"Zachariah, do you know what your problem is?" she said, her voice trembling at times. "You think you can do everything all by yourself. Nobody can do that. Even the great Dr. Jackson needs a bunch of helpers to perform successful surgeries. It's all about teamwork. A family is like a team, and its members should work together. After you thought of Dr. Jackson, you should have asked for my help. I know Dr. Jackson, and as a nurse, I have experience in dealing with all sorts of patients. I should have helped you approach Gem's dad."

An irritated Zach repeated in a determined voice, "I just wanted to be Gem's only helper."

"You're so frustrating."

"Melissa, the boy is growing up. I have a feeling he wants more independence."

Mrs. Higgins gave her husband a dumbfounded look. Awkward silence hovered over the room as the three reflected on the last statement. Zach's mom seemed baffled and overwhelmed. She moved her eyes back and forth between her husband and her son before saying, "Well, it's wrong to go places without his parents' knowledge and permission."

"You're right," replied his father. "I bet, deep down, he was uncomfortable with what he did, and that's why he wrote this confessional letter."

"Yeah, that's right," confirmed Zach.

"What about your Facebook shenanigans, pretending to be other people and dying from I don't know what?"

"He's being punished for it. You don't have to chase him with it to the grave."

Zach's mom stood up, threw her arms into the air, and walked down the hall towards her room. Her distressed face and defeated walk moved a certain something inside Zach. He followed her.

"Mom, I'm very sorry for all the wrong things I've done," he said, remorseful.

She turned around as he wrapped his arms around her. She hugged him back and whispered, "It's okay."

CHAPTER 25

Thursday, July 21

For the past three weeks, Zach had been working hard on finding funny wrestling videos to send Gem but had not received any messages from her. Even Keisha and Amanda were not very active, posting only a few negative comments. Amanda once asked why he kept sending these lame links that nobody liked. Of course, only Gem knew the answer to this question. He was just following Gem's instructions and was anxious to find out her opinion and her updates. Sometimes he thought about calling Gem, at least to ask about her dad, but didn't want to be too pushy. He was shy, a trait exaggerated when he was tired, and he surely was exhausted at the end of days filled with dreadfully challenging sports, mocking kids, and cranky coaches.

Finally, Zach found a post on Samson's wall where Gem praised many of his videos publically for the first time, perhaps providing an answer to Amanda's question. There was also a long private message.

Gem Bardel
So sorry haven't been in touch lately. So busy. The neighbor I've been babysitting 4 told her friend about me. Now, I sometimes work 4 her friend. The neighbor told me if I looked less tough, I would get more work. She also said she only hired me cuz she was desperate and cuz Grandma Cordelia guaranteed I'd do a good job (she respects Grandma a lot). She was right. Cuz I stopped looking tough, I now have more work. I write down all my jobs in a planner, so I don't get confused.

Dad went back 4 another Dr appointment the Wednesday after the surgery. His hand is getting better. He

started hand therapy 2 weeks ago. He takes bus 8 to Saint Joseph's hand rehab place three times a week. He has maybe 4 more weeks of treatment. His improvement is kind of up and down. This worries Dad a lot. Way 2 much. It's been less than 1 month since the surgery, and he started therapy only 2 weeks ago. His fears make him moody. One minute, he's happy and cool and the next, he's cranky and a pain. I feel his hand is a little better, but he doesn't. I'm always afraid he'll get 2 frustrated and quit going to therapy. When I'm not working, I work with him on his exercises 2 make sure he does them.

Mom started a job about a week ago in the new cheese factory in Shagrana, 25 minutes west of town. It's similar 2 the job she had in Minnesota. She's happy 2 be a supervisor again and to make more money.

Please, keep on sending your links. Don't worry about the girls' comments and Amanda's question. She's just silly. I don't care anymore about agreeing with them. I just said what I wanted right on my public wall.

Tuesday

Getting a message from Gem filled mostly with good news delighted Zach. The ambiguity of her father's situation worried him. In his reply, he kept his concerns to himself.

Samson 112

Hi,

Happy 2 hear all ur good news. Ur right. Ur dad is worrying way 2 much. I think the improvement u r seeing is real. His worrying is confusing him. As long as he does his exercises, he'll get better.

Not much happening here. Just me moving from one dumb sports camp 2 another. At the end of every day, my grandmother or great aunt picks me up. When my grandmother picks me up, I spend time in her pool. When my aunt picks me up, I get a wonderful meal with tons of dessert. So far, I have done basketball, swimming, volleyball, and tennis. This week I'm doing rowing, and it sure is killing my arms.

Just now

Later that evening, distress consumed Zach as he realized that Gem was now too busy to send him regular messages. He could not understand his agony when her life was improving. Wasn't that all he wanted?

Monday, August 1

After sending his usual wrestling video to Gem, Zach decided, out of curiosity, to check on Billie and see how she was doing after the "devastating" end of her romance with Chad, her "soul mate." Since the beginning of summer vacation, her busy Facebook had been ten times more active. He skimmed through post after post of mostly unnecessary web-congesting junk. It seemed Billie was now head-over-heels in love with Paul from the swim team. Zach was vaguely aware of that slender, quiet boy because they rode the same bus to school and were in the same social studies class in sixth grade. Perhaps his silence was attractive to Billie since it allowed her to do all the talking. Membership in a sports team was a plus for Billie. At least she found somebody who lived nearby and could join her regularly at the neighborhood pool where she had been planning to meet the long forgotten Chad.

She had made her last post less than an hour ago.

Billie P.

paul is still working with me on the butterfly stroke today I was finally able 2 move a little ways in the pool before my muscles gave up. paul told me that if I practice I'll get better every day. I'm going 2 have the most toned and beautiful shoulders what else can I ask 4!!! ☺

OMG Paul is soooooooooo awesome☺ I finally found the love of my life XOXOXO

did u know his parents r French? That's why he's so romantic it's in his blood. I never knew delon was french until today when he mentioned his last name and pronounced it right

4 the longest time whenever I saw his picture and name in the yearbook I thought his last name was like that famous hippie singer bill or bob or whatever

48 minutes ago

This girl is so stupid, thought Zach, slapping his forehead. *I feel like pulling my hair. The singer is Bob Dylan.*

Zach was curious to find out how she announced the end of her relationship with the imaginary Chad, but his twenty minutes were over.

Thursday, August 4

There were still no messages from Gem, so he visited Billie's Facebook where he went all the way back to June.

Billie P.
want 2 know why me and chad were not at the community pool cuz we played a prank & moved our 1ˢᵗ date 2 the bowling alley away from ur curious eyes
it was tons of fun but the chemistry we had on Facebook was not there he was sweet and cuter than in the photo but there was no chemistry funny how the online and offline worlds can be soooooo different we had a super fun time and now we r only friends.
June 10 at 4:24 p.m.

"Wow, Billie, this time, you outdid yourself," murmured Zach.

Putting a favorable spin on the exit of fake Chad was something Zach had predicted, but Billie went beyond his expectations. She kept Chad real, added a new chapter, and ended the story on a happy note. He created Chad, but she claimed him and allowed him to exit her Facebook world with more style and less pain. Of course, in Billie's world, only wonderful, magical things happened. All the tears and hysterics over Chad's illness and imminent death and all the devastation and anger over his nonexistence were deleted and replaced by a more pleasant reality.

Zach printed both messages and showed them to his mom, attempting to prove that Billie was no longer devastated and broken hearted, but was happy with her new French-blooded, romance-dripping boyfriend. So, why should he be punished and suffer when she was having a great time?

CHAPTER 26

"Zachariah, listen to me very carefully. This is the last time I'm going to say it," his mom said, looking at him with great intensity. "You're being punished because you did something wrong. She seemed to have recovered very nicely, and I'm happy for her, but the punishment is about you and what you did. It is not about her or anybody else."

"But, Mom, can't we at least get rid of baseball camp?"

"Zachariah, your whining is going to give you more punishments. Do you understand?"

He ducked his head and went back to his room.

Thursday, September 1

After weeks of faithfully sending Gem a wrestling video every Monday and Thursday, Zach received, for the first time, public compliments from Gem on most of his videos and a private message.

> **Gem Bardel**
> I saw U Tuesday evening during the Get-Ready-4-School Night. I wanted 2 say hi at the end, but U were on the opposite side of the auditorium. The aisles were so packed with people trying 2 leave, I couldn't get 2 U.
>
> Dad's hand is great. He'll start a new job on the first day of school. He'll be working at a big dealership. He'll make more money than before and have health insurance too.
>
> This Labor Day weekend, we'll move out of Grandma's apartment. My parents rented a house near her apartment. We will stay close 2 her without being like in her face all the time. The house is big. It has 3 bedrooms and 2 bathrooms. No more sleeping in the kitchen and no more long lines in front of the

bathroom door.
See U around.

4 hours ago

Gem's news cheered Zach up. Having so much to say and little time left, he typed his reply as quickly as he could.

Samson 112
Thought that was u on Tuesday. U r right. Going from one side 2 the other in that jammed auditorium was impossible. Everybody was trying 2 leave. Don't blame them 4 wanting 2 GET OUT after an hour of blabber. Why do they even have this thing every year? Why do we have 2 be introduced 2 all the 8th-grade teachers? We'll get to meet them soon enough. Instead of this stupid meeting, they should mail the schedules and locker information 2 us. End of story.

Well, I need 2 stop blabbering. So happy 4 ur dad and ur family and u. Happy u will sleep in a bedroom. Finally, free from sleeping in the kitchen.

Just now

After logging off, he wondered what kind of person a worry-free Gem would be like?

CHAPTER 27

Tuesday, September 6

Zach's alarm clock went off at 6:15 a.m., announcing the beginning of a new school year. He craved to sleep just a few more minutes. He pulled the sheets over his head, trying to muffle the insistent wails, wishing he could throw the clock out the window, so it would break into a million pieces upon contact with the ground, and would never, ever bother him again. Sadly, it was all wishful thinking. Last night, he had forgotten the clock on top of the desk, too far to grab without getting out of bed. Even if he smashed it, one of his parents would shortly show up to ensure he was awake.

Soon enough, his mother walked in, turned off the clock, and opened the curtains. Sickly rays of sun barely penetrating the thick clouds came through, giving the room a hazy glow, far from the warm, bright, energizing sun the weatherman had promised the previous night.

"Zachariah, rise and shine," said his mom with her annoying, exaggerated cheerfulness.

"Zach, please call me Zach."

"Zach sounds choppy and abrupt. Za/cha/ri/ah is so musical."

Even after his mom left, inside his head, he screamed Zach, Zach, Zach... He dragged himself out of bed and threw on whatever was the easiest to grab out of the closet.

***

The bus was more crowded than usual. Many kids hauled extra bags of school supplies. This year, he acted smart and delivered all his supplies to his locker on the Get-Ready-4-School Night. During the ride, he caught a few glimpses of the king of romance, Paul Delon, Billie's great love. Slender with long arms and legs, he lounged in his seat, listening to his iPod as if he were in a fancy hotel lobby. When they got close to the school, Zach saw a sea of students. The reality of returning to school hit him full force. He cringed.

Oh boy, he thought. *Here we go again.*

***

Zach immediately went to his locker. Kneeling, he opened it and retrieved what he needed for his first class. He then struggled to cram his backpack inside. As he slammed the locker shut, he heard, "Hey!"

He turned his head and looked up. There stood Gem, smiling, her hair one solid color of black, pulled up in a ponytail.

"Hey, Gem," he replied, smiling back as he stood up from his kneeling position.

"I guess, we're back," she said.

"I guess so."

She looked at him, her eyes wide and bright with amusement, making him self-conscious. Awkward silence hovered over them.

"You look different," she said, breaking the silence.

"I grew three inches over the summer," he said proudly, tilting his head back slightly to look her straight in the eye. He was happy he did not have to tilt his head all the way back like he had to do last year whenever he dared look her in the eye.

"I had a big growth spurt in the summer between fifth and sixth grade," replied Gem. "But, no, it's not that."

As she examined him again, he noticed she looked different, too. Her trademark faded black leather vest was gone. Instead, she was wearing a plain yellow T-shirt and a denim skirt. Was that gloss on her lips, eye shadow on her lids, and mascara on her lashes? She looked girly, but he was way too shy to comment on her looks, so he kept his observations to himself.

"I can't tell what it is," she finally said, sounding frustrated. "Maybe you look somehow more grown up or something. Oh, Zachariah, I don't know."

Gem didn't know, but he knew. He didn't look like a floppy ragdoll anymore. Thanks to all the sports camps over the summer, he was more muscular and more toned. However, talking about his muscles was too awkward and embarrassing to even consider, so Zach kept his thoughts to himself.

"How was your move?" he asked, changing the subject.

"Great. I feel so rested," she said, stretching her arms. "I slept in a bedroom on my own air mattress that I bought with my own money. No more lumpy roll-away beds; no more people drinking in the middle of the night; no more Grandmas moaning, groaning, fidgeting with coffee makers at dawn. It was the best sleep I had in my life."

"I had a good sleep until the stupid alarm clock woke me up. One day, I'm going to sell it on eBay. You wait and see."

They both laughed as the first bell rang, signaling that classes would start in five minutes.

"Zachariah, would you like to come with me to the school dance next Friday?"

Quickly, without much thinking, he accepted her invitation.

"Great," she said, grinning with satisfaction.

Now, because her hair was pulled back and he could see her face, he noticed how pretty she was. Her features were perfect, and her eyes shone blue like the sky on a bright sunny day.

As they walked in opposite directions down the hall, he realized that for the first time since the end of second grade, being called Zachariah didn't bother him. Actually, it was kind of, sort of, musical: Za/cha/ri/ah.

THE END

ABOUT THE AUTHOR

A researcher, dietitian, and diabetes specialist turned author, A. S. Wood lives in Tulsa, Oklahoma, with her husband, two sons, and a goofy cat. She won honorable mention in the 77th Annual *Writer's Digest* Writing Competition in the mainstream/literary short story category for "That Tamed Viking." A poem, "Urban PMS Rendition," and a short story, "Consent in October," appeared in *Underground Voices* and *Down in the Dirt* online literary magazines, respectively. In 2017, **she won third place in historical fiction novel for *Swaying with the Wind* from Oklahoma Writers' Federation Inc**. She has also developed the contents of a website, diabetesbitsandpieces(dot)info. In her spare time, she likes to read, cook, and walk while listening to audio books.

In middle and high school, A. S. was bullied relentlessly. Those were hard years, but she managed to survive. When her oldest son started middle school, she heard stories about bullying. That motivated her to write a novel dealing with bullying. Research followed, and she recognized the complexities and intricacies of bullying. Her experience with bullying and her research were instrumental in writing the novel.